Wint

Ghostly Tale

D.B. Carter
Derek R. King
S.J. Lomas
Natalie Reeves-Billing

8N PUBLISHING

Winter Chills

8N Publishing, LLC
P.O. Box 972364
Ypsilanti, MI 48197

Cover concept and design by Sarah Perry

Print ISBN: 978-0-9992523-1-4
Ebook available

CONTENTS

Acknowledgments   6

1   Departures and Arrivals   11

2   The Christmas Card   33

3   The Holiday Party   59

4   The Carolers   91

5   Defying Convention   105

6   Go With the Wind   121

ACKNOWLEDGMENTS

D.B. Carter: Since I've started my journey as a writer, family and friends, old and new, have supported me all the way. Here are a few to whom I send my deepest thanks: Mary, Chloe, Lyndsey, Maia, Shannon, Erin, Carly, Michele, Sara, Stephen, Mark, Rod, Leanne, Veronica, Fiona, Nikki, and Jocelyn. Your encouragement means the world.

And special thanks to my old English teacher, the late and great Mr. Edwards (known affectionately as 'Spud') who nurtured my lifelong love of literature.

Derek R. King: [Clears throat and looks down at his inky fingers holding his trusty fountain pen nicknamed "Excalibur."]

Back in early July, when my Twitter bud @jardshieI told me "I want to read fiction from you," I knew it had to be done.

So I was, and am, honoured to have been invited by 8N Publishing to contribute to this collection of seasonal short ghost stories. I have to say it's been a delight working with 8N on this project. So big thanks to 8N for that.

I'm also hugely privileged to feature in a collection featuring Natalie Reeves-Billing, S.J. Lomas, and D.B. Carter. Superb writers all.

I need to say a thank you to my lovely wife, Maree for keeping me fuelled up with tea when she'd rather be doing something else.

Most importantly, I want to thank you, the reader, for allowing me and my co-authors, into your world, home, and to sneak a little bit of your valuable time from this mad world we inhabit. I do hope you enjoy our efforts and your feedback is always welcome. As Indie Authors, it's support from folks like you that helps keep us going. So thanks again, and to you and yours I wish you all the very best. [Slumps back in chair, places Excalibur on desk, picks up drink.]

"Slàinte Mhath"

S.J. Lomas: This book would not be in existence without the help and incredible support of Jeff Perry, Jane Lomas, Monica Anderson, Heather Hollister, and Jody Lamb. Thanks go to Patty and Ted for being awesome and patient, most of the time.

D.B. Carter, Derek R. King, and Natalie Reeves-Billing, I am so proud to be in a book alongside you. You're great writers and wonderful people. Thank you for doing this project with me.

Really, huge thanks go to YOU. Since you're reading this, you made the decision to buy the book and go on the journey the authors have laid out for you. This, more than anything, is what a writer dreams of. I hope you enjoy the stories as much as we enjoyed writing them for you.

Natalie Reeves-Billing: The Winter Chills as Christmas approaches. In keeping with that, I'll unwrap my thanks like a well-wrapped present.

To all our readers, and the beautiful supporters within the #WritingCommunity, particularly my coop siblings, the #WriteChickens, thank you. I'm indebted to you all.

To my fellow authors. S.J. Lomas, DB Carter, and Derek King, we are bound together, literally and figuratively, for an eternity.

To my mum, Linda Reeves, Su Taylor, Lynn Howden, Julie Fife, Clare Coombes. Thanks for sticking with me through various redrafts and edits. I'll never forget that.

And as I tear through the final layer, thank you to my long-suffering husband, Colin Billing, and my little monsters Nathaniel and Ellie-Rose. I hope this short story is worth that empty seat at the dinner table. I

love you more than even my finest analogies could
ever describe.

D.B. Carter lives with his family on the edge of a small town nestled amongst the rolling hills of rural Devon, England.

The son of two nomadic artists, he grew up in a world of creativity, studying painting techniques under his parents' tutelage. In his 20s, he went to university and followed a career in science and later commerce, running his own business for twenty years.

A lifelong bibliophile, he is firmly of the opinion that there is no such thing as too many books, only insufficient shelf space; it was his love of classical literature, of Dickens and Brontë, that led to the creation of "The Cherries."

His philosophy is, "If we look for the good, we will find it."

BOOKS BY D.B. CARTER

The Cherries
The Wild Roses

Departures and Arrivals

by: D.B. Carter

How could it be so dark when the snow was so white? Holly could barely see more than a few feet in front of her as she stumbled over unseen obstacles beneath the crisp covering on the ground; yet she pressed on, icy flakes weighing heavy on her eyelashes and cold dampness infiltrating her thin coat. English winters weren't supposed to be like this – a bit of snow, yes, but this was a heavy blizzard.

It was a blessing that she knew the route so well, because she walked it every day at the start of her commute. Gradually a pinkish yellow light began to show and she at last stumbled onto the railway station platform. Ironically, out of the snow and under the awning that jutted out in front of the tired building, it was colder than ever. Holly shook uncontrollably, and she hugged her arms.

Unbelievably, the waiting room light was on. The station should have been locked up long ago at 11pm on Christmas Eve, with tickets only available from a soulless machine, but it seemed fate had other plans.

Holly pushed the door open and stepped inside, blinking under the harsh fluorescent light humming overhead. Nerves overtook her, as if she were a mischievous child entering a forbidden place, and she adopted her familiar hunched posture, ready to utter profuse apologies for intruding. But there was no one there, and her self-loathing abated sufficiently to allow herself the comfort of one of the rounded red metal benches. She perched nervously on the edge of the seat, too cold and numb to think, other than checking the large clock on the wall. It was 11:07 – she had 53 minutes until the train.

The door rattled as the wind outside picked up and the snow changed from a steady vertical stream of flakes to a thousand swirls and eddies dancing to the storm's tune, glittering in the lights on the platform.

"You look cold, love."

Holly jumped and turned in her seat to see a tall woman standing before her. Her skin was weathered to leather and her teeth were discoloured with several gaps. Over her substantial girth, a tatty grey jumper was just the first layer of clothing, as several equally dishevelled cardigans progressed towards a heavy waterproof overcoat. She had an oversized floral skirt atop misshapen corduroy trousers, which were tucked into some newish looking wellington boots. Her head was protected from the elements by a knitted headpiece under a broad-brimmed felt hat. Pieces of newspaper protruded from various items of clothing, where they had been expertly stuffed, and crackled when she moved. The sights and the sounds were one thing, but the stench was another – it was quite overpowering in the confines of the waiting room.

Holly stared dumbly, unable to process the words the woman had spoken.

"I said you look cold," the woman repeated. She gestured to a stack of newspapers on a low table at the back of the room. "That's the local paper, it's free and it's warm, if you take my drift."

"Um," Holly's eyes darted to the papers and back to the bright blue eyes beneath the prematurely wrinkled brow. "Thank you."

"What are you doing here anyway?"

"I'm waiting for the midnight train."

"Really? It must be a Christmas special; it doesn't normally stop here at that time." The woman's face creased even more as she seemingly wrestled with a dilemma. "Well, if there are going to be folk coming and going, I'm making myself scarce. But I've a right to be here, you know."

"I'm sure you have."

"I just don't want porters and the like causing a ruckus and asking me my business. Honestly, on tonight of all nights, I thought I'd have some peace in here." The woman reached behind a bench and collected together an oddment of carrier bags, stuffed full of what Holly assumed were her worldly possessions. Within moments, she had fumbled the door open and walked out, to be replaced by a blast of bleak winter air.

"Where will you go?" Holly asked, long after the door closed. She cared what happened to the woman. She reproached herself for not telling her to stay – but she needed to be alone while she waited for the train that would not stop.

Oh, she was so cold and so sad and both bit into her bones and soul like ravenous demons. The clock chimed the quarter hour – strange to have such an old clock still in use.

And then, to emphasize the bleakness of her state, the lights went out. The storm must have taken down the power lines, Holly supposed, but the temperature in the room dropped so quickly that such reasoning was replaced by a desire to control her shivering. She edged her way to the back of the room and felt for a newspaper – maybe the advice would work, maybe it would keep her warm. For a little while at least – it didn't need to last long. Just until midnight when the train would be there.

Holly clasped the paper in her hands and edged back towards her bench but froze before she got there. A man's footsteps were on the platform outside, one step heavy, the second lighter and that foot scraped on the ground. Closer and closer they came, and Holly watched him pass the window and stop at the door.

A peaked cap was all she could discern, and she assumed it was the porter. But he paused to light a cigarette, and in the glow of the match Holly saw a scarred, once handsome face and the khaki uniform of a soldier.

He resumed his walk and pushed open the door – Holly struggled to understand why she could still see his face, see all of him, despite the lack of light. He stood on the threshold and stared straight at her with pale dead eyes.

"Is that you, Ivy?" he asked.

"No," Holly's voice sounded thin as a mouse's squeak when it echoed around the waiting room.

The man stepped forward, squinting like a suspicious predator.

"I suppose you ain't – but why stand in the dark?"

"The lights went out a couple of minutes ago."

The soldier drew on his cigarette and exhaled, bathing Holly in tobacco fumes.

"Yeah? Well they never were up to much, out here. Got no matches?"

"No, I don't smoke."

"Oh, right," the man withdrew a box from his tunic, struck a sizzling flame from a match, and peered around the room before walking smartly to an oil lamp hanging on the wall.

"That's odd," Holly frowned. "I don't remember seeing that before. Don't waste your time - it must be decorative; they wouldn't leave something like that in here if it had any fuel in it."

She fell silent when the rich yellow light from the lamp began to fill the room. The soldier gestured to a bench and Holly found herself sitting down, hunched in a self-hug of misery and cold; she jumped perceptibly when, having placed the lamp on the bench opposite, he sat beside her, straight-backed and immobile except for the occasional movement of his arm, traced by the satanic glow of the cigarette.

The smell of tobacco and burning oil was nauseating and Holly silently willed the lights to flicker back on, but she felt another wave of misery and despair wash over her and almost ceased to care. Almost. Eventually, lost in a world of sadness and unaware of the passing of time but marking each tick of the old clock, irritation burst through when her companion lit a new cigarette.

"I wish they'd get a bloody move on with the electricity!"

"Nah," said the soldier. "Not for hours yet. It's too unreliable out this way. That's why they keep the oil lamps."

"Really?" Holly's surprise manifested itself as a note of indignant rebuttal. "I use this station nearly every day, and I've never had a problem. It's probably just the snow."

"What snow? It's icy, I grant you, but not a cloud to be seen." The man tilted his head with feline ease. "What have you been drinking?"

"Look, I…" but Holly tailed off as she looked out of the still open door that she was sure had been closed before they sat down. There was no snow falling and none on the ground beyond the platform awning. "I don't understand."

"Blimey, you must have had a skinful." The soldier smirked as he walked to the door, pushed it shut and returned to his seat. The thin, oily black fumes coiling up from the old lamp swirled briefly, disturbed by the door closing, and hung in the cold air as the amber flames danced macabre shadows on the walls.

"I'm not drunk… just confused."

"A fag clears the airways and the brain – sure you don't want one?" A cigarette packet was waved in Holly's direction.

"No, thank you. Anyway, you're not allowed to smoke in here."

"Who told you that?"

"No one. It's illegal."

"You must think I was born yesterday. They'd have a bloody riot if they tried that. Anyway, if you're so keen about the law, where's your gas mask?"

Holly's head was beginning to throb, and she was sure that it was to do with the polluted atmosphere, thick with cigarette smoke and noxious fumes from the oil lamp. But something in the soldier's words troubled her and she pushed through the cotton wool clouds in her mind and grappled a question to her lips.

"Gas Mask?"

"We've all got to carry them. Where have you been hiding this last year?" The soldier peered at her once more. His demeanour became aggressive and his eyes blazed with suspicion. "Maybe you're a spy."

Holly blinked to wake herself, but her eyelids felt like lead. The oppressive air made her hot, even though it was a midwinter night and the waiting room was rapidly cooling. She battled to make sense of the situation – why was this strange man acting like someone from eighty years ago, from when that lamp was young? Then an explanation presented itself.

"Oh, you're one of those re-enactment people, aren't you?"

A humourless smile spread slowly across the soldier's pale thin lips. He snorted – was it a mocking laugh? - and resumed a more genial attitude.

"Am I? I suppose I am. Yes – yes, I like that. I'm doing some… re-enactment."

Reassured, Holly relaxed into her seat and took her phone from her pocket. The screen bathed her face in blue-white light, and it took some moments for her eyes to adjust. There was no reception and no Wi-Fi (of course, how could there be in a power cut?) but hopes of messages having come through before she was cut off were dashed. Her sense of isolation increased as she returned the useless device to her pocket.

"I'm Andrew," the soldier suddenly volunteered.

"Holly," she replied. Her natural reticence was overpowered partly by innate politeness but mainly because knowing his name humanised the strange young man.

"My Ivy will be here soon," Andrew said.

The clock struck the quarter-to chimes, and Holly frowned.

"What happened to half past?"

"You were asleep."

"No, no I wasn't… was I?"

Andrew never got to reply, as the door opened, blasting a wave of freezing air over the two occupants of the waiting room. A tall man stood on the threshold; his features were shrouded by shadow, but the uniform he wore was unmistakably that of a railway employee from the mid-20th Century. Holly presumed him to be another re-enactment enthusiast and was almost grateful to him for the cold breeze which revived her.

"Good evening. It's a cold night tonight." The newcomer's voice was soft and silky – more of a hiss than whisper.

"Good evening, Mr. Proctor," Andrew seemed positively excited. "If you're here, my Ivy soon will be."

"Why, yes. She'll be along when your friend here's train arrives."

"Me?" Holly realised that both men were smiling at her. "There's a mistake, the train doesn't stop."

"We know that. No need to worry," Mr. Proctor smiled. His body had a serpentine sway and Holly presumed he had stopped off for some seasonal good will at the local pub. "It won't be long now, so I'd better be about my business."

"I think I'll be off," Holly said, standing up.

"No, stay, for a bit," Mr. Proctor oiled. "It's freezing out there."

He stepped out of the door and closed it firmly behind him.

"Yes, stay," Andrew said, a note of worry tangible in his voice.

"But I was here for privacy, not for company. There was something I needed to do but I wanted to be alone."

"That's fine. After all, we're all alone in the end," Andrew's expression became introspective, as if he were remembering a long-passed event. "I was."

Holly continued to the door and turned the handle, but it would not budge. She thought it stuck until she realised the point of resistance was beside the lock. Mr. Proctor must have had a key.

"I can't open it," she said, her voice sharp with anxiety.

"Proctor will be back for you soon enough, when it's time."

Andrew resumed smoking and stared ahead, but Holly was unwilling to accept the status quo.

"Hello!" she shouted, rattling the door and banging on its glass panel. "You've locked me in. I need to leave."

In the gloom of the platform, she was sure she could see a man standing by the office entrance. Then the shadow moved through the door and within a few moments the station loudspeakers crackled to life… but that was impossible because there was a power cut. Proctor's voice reverberated around the frozen station.

"Good evening, ladies and gentlemen. The non-stop express will shortly be passing through. There will be one arrival and one departure."

"What the hell is he on about?" Holly felt her chest constrict with anxiety and she thumped the glass once more, more out of frustration than an effort to get Proctor's attention. She turned to the soldier. "He's locked us in, don't you care? And what does he mean about arrivals and departures? The train doesn't stop."

Andrew slowly turned his head and smirked a sickly smile, "He'll let us out when it's the right time, don't you worry. You won't miss the train."

"Miss the—what are you on about?"

Before any answer came, the speakers crackled again. An unfamiliar hum slowly resolved itself into the voice of a woman.

"It's so dark here," the voice wailed, "I'm so alone. Andrew, Andrew are you there? Are you still there?"

"Yes, Ivy," the soldier replied. "I'm here, I can hear you, Ivy. I hear your voice, my love."

"It's so dark, I can't see you. Where are you? Hold me!"

"I can't yet, my love. Soon. You'll arrive here soon."

"But it's been so long. It's been eighty Christmases."

Holly stared at the soldier who was now walking towards her.

"It's alright, Ivy," he said. "This time there is a willing replacement. She's waiting."

"Why is she willing? Why does she want to be here, Andy? There's something here with me – evil it is, and it keeps me here. I can't see it, but I sense it. It won't let me go to the light."

"You mustn't go into the light, Ivy. You've got to come back here with me."

Holly watched in disbelief as the soldier turned the handle of the formerly locked door and it swung open with ease. She gasped as even colder air stabbed her lungs, "What are you talking about?"

"You – you're here to help us, aren't you? Eighty years I've been waiting for Ivy, and at last you've come. Mr. Proctor explained everything to me."

"You are bloody mad!" Holly backed through the door onto the platform and turned to run, only to meet the broad chest and blue tunic of Mr. Proctor. Two ice cold hands gripped her arms, and she struggled. "Let me go!"

"I'll not be denied!" Andrew shouted, his face contorted. "Not after eighty of these nights."

"Eighty of what nights?"

Andrew's fury burst forth and he tore open his tunic. Holly stopped struggling and stared at the soldier's body. A large chuck of his torso was missing, like it had been bitten away. Certainly, no one could survive such an injury.

"What happened to you?" she asked, revolted. "What the hell is this?"

"He died, that's what," Ivy's voice cut in like the cold of the night. "He died messing around with his army buddies, never stopped to think of me and the baby."

"Shut up!" Andrew screamed.

"He went to fight for King and Country and never got past the training camp," Ivy's voice was a mixture of timeless grief and weary anger. "Blew himself up playing a prank. On Christmas Eve of all days."

"I said shut up!"

"You left me and Wendy."

"I never!" Andrew's voice lost its anger and was just a pathetic squeal of hurt. "I came home, didn't I?"

Holly's initial shock subsided, and forgetting to be scared, she asked, "How? How could anyone come back from those injuries?"

"Just lucky, I guess." Now Andrew was sulking.

"Not enough. Tell me," Holly insisted.

As soon as she spoke, Proctor tightened his grip on her arms, hissing, "Be silent. The train will be here soon."

Ivy's voice crackled from the speakers once again, "The thing that came home wasn't my Andrew."

"It was me; this is me!"

"No – a part of you, Andy, but not you. Just the angry, scared, hating part of you. That's why I ran."

"You left our child, you left our Wendy," Andrew was now the accuser.

"You think I don't know that? You think I willingly went?"

"You came here on Christmas night and you jumped in front of the midnight train. Why Ivy?"

"Better an orphan than the child of a monster. You're tied to me, not her. But it's taken you eighty Christmases to ask," Ivy laughed with arid emotion. "Every time, it takes a while for the memories to come back – but they always do. And I remember everything."

Holly was fighting for breath as she watched and listened. Proctor's grip on her arms seemed to coil around her body and squeeze the air from her lungs.

"Please let me go," she whispered. "I don't belong here. I just want to go home."

"You said she was willing," Ivy's statement hung like an accusation.

Andrew looked at Proctor in confused agitation.

"You said she was willing," he echoed.

"Be silent all of you – the train is but a minute away," Proctor growled.

"Why did you come here? I must have the truth," the soldier asked Holly.

"My sister, Beth," she replied and then hesitated, dragging back a painful memory. "Christmas Eve last year… she… came here and killed herself. It's such a painful memory, I had to be here… on the station… where she stood… at that exact moment before she... I didn't know, you see, I didn't understand. I miss her so much, I—"

Holly's words were crushed away by Proctor's unnatural embrace. Andrew stared at him. In the distance, a train whistle sounded.

"I'll have no more innocents die for me!" Ivy cried out. "They're always supposed to be the one and they never are."

"Have they all been lies and tricks?" Andrew demanded of Proctor.

"We must keep going, my boy."

"When you found me on that field, you asked what I'd give to survive, and I said I'd sell my soul to the devil himself if I could get home to my Ivy and our little Wendy."

"And I kept my end of the bargain."

"This is wrong!" Holly screamed, when the lights of the train appeared in the distance. "Please help me, Andrew!"

"I can't, he owns me. I gave him my soul, and he owns me. He – you – are my only way of getting my Ivy back."

"It's been eighty years, Andy. We don't belong in the world any more," said the voice on the loudspeaker. "What would we be anyway? What would I be? Like you? Not alive and not whole."

The sound of the locomotive grew louder. Holly could make out the black smoke and the hellish glow from the fires of the steam engine.

"He doesn't own you, because you can't sell what's not yours to give," Holly shouted to Andrew as Porter dragged her to the edge of the platform. The unseen coils tightened, and the last breath was forced from her body.

"Help her!" Ivy told her love. "You and I decided our own lots – no more of this. Be my Andy, be the man I wed on that happy June day."

Andrew calmed. A decision was made. Like a mongoose on a cobra, he launched himself at Proctor, who was obliged to release Holly. She collapsed to the platform and struggled to get air back into her lungs; looking back, she saw the two men wrestling as the train burst into the station.

Then, Andrew stood back. For an agonising moment Porter teetered on the edge of the platform, his eyes a blaze of reptilian fury, before he fell backwards beneath the merciless iron wheels of the train. Holly fancied she heard an inhuman scream over the cacophony of the steam engine passing by. She struggled to her feet.

Silence returned and Andrew stared at the blackness where the track lay.

"What have I done?" he asked.

"The right thing," Holly replied.

"But my Ivy!"

"No, my love," the voice on the speakers crackled. "It's time for us to be together somewhere else. The beast has gone – I'm going to the light."

"No, no, there must be another way."

"But it's beautiful, I'll be waiting Andy… Oh my…"

The speakers fell silent.

"Thank you," Holly called out. Then she repeated it to Andrew. "Thank you, you saved me."

"No," he replied, "I think you saved me."

A hundred thousand tiny dots of light came from within him and surrounded him. Holly finally discerned his features, young and unscarred, smiling.

"Ivy," he said, "I see you."

Holly began to weep, she looked away, knowing this departure was not for her eyes to see. But then seventy-nine voices cracked over the speakers, each saying "Thank you." The last to speak was one she knew. She sank to her knees and sobbed, not noticing the snow falling or the station lights flickering on once more.

A hand touched her shoulder.

"You OK, Holly?"

"Beth?" Holly jumped to her feet and hugged her sister. "How are you here?"

"I followed your tracks in the snow, until it was obvious you were coming here. But why?"

"Why? Because you…" Holly trailed off unable to process anything, to realise anything except elation.

"I woke up from the worst nightmare, and you were gone," Beth said. "Oddly, this station was in it. Then I was suddenly in the dark, and I was being kept there by something evil I couldn't see. I felt I had to find you, sis. I knew you'd understand."

"I do, I promise I do," Holly hugged Beth again. "Goodness, it's cold. Let's head home."

The two young women walked arm in arm, towards the house they shared, both happier than they could imagine ever having been before. As they trudged into the village centre, past the old church with the multicoloured lights hanging on the Christmas tree outside, to the welcome glow of the streetlamps, the snowfall started to ease off. The pristine white that covered cars and bushes filled them with childish joy.

They decided simultaneously to stop and make snowballs. The first two struck a post box, but then a joyous sibling fight started, with handfuls of white powder being hurled amid youthful giggles. A wayward ball struck the back of the bench by the bus stop and brought forth a loud harrumph from the darkness.

"Is someone there?" Holly asked.

"You again," a woman's voice replied, and the old lady from the waiting room walked into the circle of light from the streetlamp. "You seem determined to interrupt me this evening."

"I am so sorry," Holly said, and Beth echoed the sentiment.

"You may have done me a favour, actually. I can head back to the station. Is the waiting room still open?"

"I didn't check – sorry."

"I think I'll go and see." The elderly lady started to gather her bags together. "Happy Christmas, I suppose."

"Oh, yes, it's Christmas," the sisters chorused. "Merry Christmas to you too."

They watched the hunched figure walk away.

"Wait!" Holly called and she glanced at Beth, who nodded. "Our house is close by, it's much warmer. Will you join us for Christmas?"

"Why?"

"Because, we'd like your company. We don't have our mum and dad any more."

"I never did – orphaned as a baby. OK, I'll come. Not for long mind – but it is chilly, and I'd not say no to a cuppa. I'm over eighty, you know."

"I'm Holly and this is my sister, Beth."

"Pleased to meet you," said the old woman as she joined the younger women on the walk home.

"So, what's your name?" Holly asked.

"Wendy."

"Then come home with us, Wendy. Merry Christmas."

The Christmas Card

by: D.B. Carter

Phil's morning was going according to
schedule, though he had only been up for half an hour.
He had awoken refreshed when his alarm had gone
off and managed to be shaved and dressed before his
wife, Jo had even managed to leave the warm
sanctuary of their bed.

He could hear her upstairs as he started to
make breakfast. The kettle was empty, and he filled it
from the tap, only to hear Jo squawk and then shout
strict instructions to either get new plumbing in their
old house or to not use the cold tap when someone
was showering. Fearing spousal reprisals may

otherwise take place the next day, he went to the foot of the stairs and yelled platitudes.

There was a rattle from the post box and several envelopes collectively thudded onto the doormat. Phil picked them up and sorted the items as he went back into the kitchen to finish making coffee. Bills, a postcard from a work colleague who had sent it whilst on holiday three weeks ago, an "amazing offer" from his broadband provider which was worse than the one they already gave him, and a large, mysterious envelope that clearly contained a card. It was addressed to both of them, but Phil suspected it was a wedding invitation and thought Jo would rather open it.

Absorbed by eating muesli and scrolling his Twitter feed, Phil had quite forgotten about the post by the time Jo walked into the kitchen looking pristine.

"What's this?" she asked, picking up the mysterious envelope.

"I assumed it was an invitation to something. Isn't your niece Ella getting married?"

Jo tore open the envelope and pulled out the contents.

"Oh, it's a Christmas Card," she laughed.

"It's only just gone Halloween," Phil said. "Someone's a bit keen. Who's it from?"

"It says, 'To Jo and Phil, Hoping you have a Christmas you won't forget, Samantha'."

"Do we know a Samantha?"

"No one I can think of… well no one who would send us a card, or who'd know our address." Jo racked her brain. "Actually, the only Samantha I've ever known who didn't shorten her name would be the last person on earth who'd send one. Hang on a minute, though – weren't you always talking about a Samantha at work a while back?"

"That was ages ago, and she worked for a supplier."

"Well, whoever it is, they have lovely writing. Proper calligraphy, so they must have taken ages. I feel terrible that I don't know who sent it." Jo peered at the front of the card. It featured a typical Victorian living room, with husband and wife posing either side of the fireplace and a Christmas tree in the corner. "You know, I can't tell if it's a photo or a painting. The colours are so rich."

"If it's in colour, it may be a hand-tinted photo." Phil peered over his wife's shoulder. "I see what you mean though, it looks more like an oil painting. Amazing resolution, though. Maybe it's a modern picture done through a filter of some kind. Clever stuff."

Jo peered closer. "Look on the mantelpiece, there is a copy of the card next to the clock. That's a fun trick."

"Well, it must be modern, then."

"Or it is a painting," Jo said, holding the card at arm's length and tilting her head appreciatively, "but to get that level of detail is incredible. This is getting pride of place in the living room."

"Where? You've got everything so minimalist in there that you've got nothing to put it on."

"It can sit on the coffee table until we decide." Jo walked through the hallway to the lounge. "You know, I suppose this room looked quite like the one in the picture when it was new."

"Before you spent a fortune having everything ripped out," Phil laughed. "Speaking of money, we've got jobs to go to. Come on, you can drop me at the station on your way."

The rain was lashing down when Phil travelled home from work and the last walk from the station to the house was pure misery. He clattered through the front door and stood in the hallway, dripping and not wanting to move because his clothes were uncomfortably wet when next to his skin. He unclenched his frozen fingers long enough for his briefcase to thud to the floor, and wrestled out of his mac, which had long given up any pretence of protecting him from the deluge outside.

"Are you home, Jo?" he called out as he kicked off his shoes. It was a rhetorical question because the car was parked outside, so she must be there. "Jo! Jo, are you here?"

Still no reply. Maybe she had popped next door to see their neighbour. He kicked off his sodden shoes and nudged them to dry under the radiator. For a moment, Phil hesitated – should he go upstairs and change or make a hot drink first? He squelched to the staircase and then froze, one hand on the banister; a woman's voice was quietly humming the same short sequence of notes over and over. The tune was so slow and so contorted that it took several seconds of careful listening to discern they were the opening bars of 'Ding Dong Merrily on High'.

Gently, Phil pushed open the living room door and saw his wife standing staring at the mysterious Christmas card, oblivious to his presence and humming the eerie tune.

"Jo!"

She looked up with a startled jump.

"Hello, darling. I didn't hear you come in."

"Obviously. Do me a favour and stick the kettle on while I go up and change, will you? I'm freezing."

"OK, but hurry up because there's something I want to talk to you about."

Phil nodded and jogged upstairs to peel off his suit and sling on a pair of chinos, the warmest socks he could find, and a heavy sweater. When he arrived in the kitchen, Jo handed him a cup of tea.

"I've had a great idea," she said, bubbling with excitement. "I'm going to do a Victorian themed Christmas this year. You know, old fashioned decorations, and maybe we could have a goose?"

"I can't see that look fitting in with the décor. What did you do last year, wasn't it purple and silver? What's wrong with doing that again?"

"Because I never do the same theme twice, you know that," Jo scolded, as if his objection was wholly unreasonable. "Anyway, I've already made a start." She gestured to the back door, beside which sat a brass coal scuttle and a matching poker set.

"Where the hell did you get them?" Phil asked. "They're hardly in keeping with the rest of the living room."

"They were in that new little antique shop that's opened up on the high street. They'll look lovely when I've finished – for heavens' sake, I'm a window dresser, Phil! I know how to do this and make it look right. The card will fit in beautifully."

"You're obsessed with that blasted Christmas card! You've not stopped going on about it all week!"

"I just think it's lovely, that's all." Hurt boiled in Jo's eyes. "I thought you liked it too."

"It is... I do," Phil said, taken aback by the strength of her reaction. "I suppose I'm just tired."

Jo brushed his chest, as if removing some invisible lint from his sweater. Her eyes met his in playful expectation.

"You know," she said, drawing out her words, "you could look on this as my Christmas present if you like, and you know how excited I get about my prezzies."

Phil placed his cup on the counter and put his arms around his wife. He nuzzled her neck.

"Oh, good boy," Jo whispered, "and I'm going to give you your present now too."

"Well, that sounds wonderful," he murmured into her ear. "But Christmas is still weeks away, I hope this won't be the last time I get to unwrap you before then."

"Oh, but this is a special present. A one-off so to speak."

A thousand exotic possibilities tantalised Phil's brain, and he slowly began moving his hands down her back while upping his neck nibbling activities. His excitement grew as she squirmed appreciatively.

"Do tell," he said, sliding his hand under her top and caressing the base of her spine. She inwardly thanked the cup of tea, because holding it had taken the chill off his fingers.

"Well," Jo bit his ear lobe, "I am going to let you…"

"Yes?"

"Grow a beard."

Phil's caresses froze. Many possibilities had whizzed through his brain before his wife said those words, and none of them had involved him growing facial hair.

"But you hate beards, you said it's like kissing a scouring pad."

"Well, that's why it's a present, silly," Jo laughed. "I think you might look rather distinguished. Just think, no more having to shave every morning."

Phil had mixed emotions. For one thing, the mood was certainly broken. For another, getting to grow a beard seemed a poor exchange of gifts when his life partner had clearly already spent quite a bit of money on her Christmas theme. As he thought, his eyes lit upon the mysterious card. He narrowed his eyes.

"The man on the card has a beard," he observed. "Is that behind this?"

Jo shuffled awkwardly and leant nonchalantly against the kitchen counter.

"I suppose he does," she said, as if only just noticing. "I say, wouldn't it be fun if we dressed up as them and took a photo just like that one?"

Phil shrugged. "I suppose so." He was confident that his wife would never want to look like the stern-faced, dowdy woman in the picture, hair scraped back into a severe bun and eyebrows scowling.

"Yes!" Jo yelped, pulling him to her. She pointed to her lips. "Now I believe you've got some work to finish off, lover boy."

Phil stopped one house early on his way home from work. Partly because he had received a text from his neighbour saying she had signed for a parcel for him, and partly because he couldn't stand the thought of getting back home to see what Jo had bought for the Christmas theme that day. The last few weeks had seen an assortment of dusty old curtains, threadbare chairs, woodworm-riddled side tables, and tarnished oil lamps strewn about the living room. Yesterday, the latest acquisition had been a once splendorous rug of burgundy and gold, which was now a faded red brown with yellow streaks and dark stains.

Carol opened the door and ushered him in.

"Want a glass of wine?" she asked. "I've just opened a Pinot Noir, and believe me I need it after the day I've had. I had to pick Polly up from school, as she's down with some bug and I've two reports I have to get finished for work."

"Nightmare," Phil sympathised. "How is she now?" He gratefully accepted the glass that was held out to him and expertly savoured the bouquet.

"Her temperature's gone, but she's still lethargic. She slept most of the day, which was a miracle after all the banging coming from your place this afternoon. You got the builders in?"

"Not that I know of," Phil frowned and sipped his drink. "But Jo's got the day off, so maybe she's working on her Christmas theme."

"Yes, it seems very grand. She's been at it for weeks. When do we get to see the finished results?"

"Well, it was a mess last time I looked," Phil laughed, scratching his chin.

"I must say that beard of yours is coming on well," Carol said, "you look quite the pirate captain."

"I suppose I should trim it, but Jo wants me to leave that until Christmas week. She wants to be sure it's authentic, whatever that means."

"I'm surprised she let you grow it. She's always been dead against them. She was aghast when I dated Mark, and he only had a moustache."

"It seems it's my Christmas present. Which reminds me, have you got my parcel?"

"Oops! I almost forgot," Carol laughed. She hurried out of the room and returned a few moments later with a small box. "What have you been ordering? Prezzies for Jo?"

"You must be joking after all she's spending on this stupid Christmas theme of hers. No, this is for me. I'm not getting any other presents other than this beard – which itches like hell, I might add – so I'm treating myself to a smartwatch. I guess I'll have to wait till I get to work tomorrow before I set it up, because Jo's not going to see the funny side if she knows I've got it. Once it's on my wrist, she'll never clock it until it's been there for ages."

"Another boy playing with his toy," Carol rolled her eyes good-naturedly. "Tell you what, stay here, finish your drink and set up your silly gadget before you go home."

By the time Phil passed through his own front door, he was less than steady on his feet. The watch had taken longer than expected to configure, and Carol had been more than generous with the contents of her wine rack.

He frowned. Strange noises came from the living room, scrapes and taps, interspersed with the same hummed bars of 'Ding Dong Merrily on High' being repeated ad nauseum. When he entered the room, he stopped short. Everything was covered in dust and debris, especially Jo who looked up from where she was skilfully installing an authentic period fireplace.

"Well?" she said, cocking her head in exultant expectation.

"Well!" Phil echoed. "Well, I'm wondering what the hell you're doing. It's hardly any time since we paid a fortune to have the old one taken out, and… wait, have you reopened the chimney?"

"Of course I have. It would look pretty stupid otherwise. It'll look lovely when I've finished."

"But what's the point?" Phil's exasperation reached volcanic overflow, aided and abetted by alcohol. "And where's the bloody TV gone?"

Their huge television was not secured to the wall as it had been that very morning.

"I put it in the garage until the New Year. You can still watch the telly in our room."

"Have you forgotten how much that TV cost? Now it's sitting among all those boxes of junk of yours in the garage that we can't even put the car in. I can't believe how stupid you've been!"

"There's no need to be like that! What was I supposed to do when Samantha told me that she heard about this going for sale? It's perfect."

"Samantha?"

"Yes, Samantha from the antique shop." Jo stopped to think for a moment, as if only just connecting the name. "Wouldn't it be funny if she was the one who sent us the card?"

"I wouldn't be surprised if it wasn't some way of drumming up business."

"Now who's being stupid?" Jo walked closer to her husband. "Ugh! You stink of alcohol, no wonder you're in a foul mood. Why don't you go up to our room and have a lie down? Watch some telly and I'll bring you up something to eat."

Phil was about to tell her what to do with her food, when he felt his new smartwatch catch on his sleeve. He aggressively kicked off his shoes and stomped upstairs to play with his new toy.

"Phil! Phil! Wait for me!"

Phil stopped walking and turned around. Carol was trotting towards him, laden with carrier bags.

"Give us a hand, will you?" she said, holding out an armful of shopping. He awkwardly took on fifty percent of her burden and they resumed walking home side by side. "I saw you on the train, but it was too crowded to get your attention."

"What do you expect on Christmas Eve?" he asked.

"Alright, Mr. Scrooge. I can see that you are full of seasonal good will."

"I'm sorry, I'm just on edge. Ever since the TV disappeared, I've been banned from my own living room."

"Oh, she's making you wait too?" Carol laughed. "Same here. She said it's got to be a surprise."

"Well, it's Christmas Eve – time for the big reveal. I've got to get dressed up like an idiot in some suit she's bought and come and join her in the living room. She's been working hard on it, so I'll not let her down. Maybe it'll be the end of her humming that stupid tune over and over."

"Well, she's looking well on the whole thing," Carol observed. "I swear she's lost weight. Her figure's never looked so good."

Phil laughed. "She's been wearing a corset for the last few weeks. Making me tighten it a bit more every day. It's for her costume."

"You are kidding me! She'll do herself an injury."

"I nearly did her an injury when I saw the credit card bill."

"That's not funny, not even a little bit."

"Sorry, I didn't think." Phil chastised himself as he recalled why Carol lived alone and in fear of her ex-husband.

"You men seldom do."

They arrived at Carol's house and Phil insisted he carry the shopping inside.

"No wine for you tonight," Carol teased. "You've got to get home."

"Yes, Jo's invited the woman from the antique shop over to see the room. She's going to take our picture, all dressed up, on an authentic camera." Phil dumped the shopping bags on the kitchen counter and then walked towards the front door.

"Do you have to go just yet?" Carol asked. She had followed him part way and was standing beneath a sprig of mistletoe. She glanced upward.

"Not again, Carol. Not tonight."

"Please," she whispered. "Polly's at her grandmothers, I'm here alone. It doesn't mean anything, Phil. I just need someone to hold me. Just for thirty seconds."

He stalked forward and placed his arms around her. Her face moved to his and their lips brushed.

"Yuck!" she laughed. "Now I know why Jo's not keen on beards."

Phil was offended. "I should have known better than to feel sorry for you."

"Don't be like that, please. I was just joking."

Phil believed he had the advantage of being the injured party. "Maybe I'll come back on Boxing Day and we can try again."

"Blimey, I don't need your favours that badly!"

"Suit yourself." Phil opened the front door.

"Wait!" Carol's voice cracked. "What time?"

"Nine. Jo's got to be at the shop dressing the window for the sale. She'll be out of the house by eight."

"OK. See you tomorrow. Thanks for inviting me."

Phil nodded and closed the door behind him. He walked briskly down Carol's driveway and up his own, dabbing a tissue against his lips in case there was a trace of lipstick. As soon as he was indoors, Jo's voice rang out from the living room. "Hurry upstairs and get changed, darling. Samantha will be here at any moment."

A dark suit was laid out on the bed, and on top of it sat a neatly wrapped box. There was a tag bearing his wife's writing.

'Thanks for putting up with me while I make this theme work. I remember what you said about wanting a new watch, and I thought this might be fun. All my love, Jo.'

He smiled – she *had* remembered. No need for her to know about the smartwatch he already had on his wrist. Now he would have two – or maybe he could sell one? He tore the paper off the package and looked in the box. An antique gold man's fob watch on a long chain stared at him. Disappointment and irritation gripped him; he was about to go downstairs and whinge when the doorbell rang, and he heard Jo answer.

Instead, Phil changed clothes. He struggled with the unfamiliar starched collar and cuffs but eventually, he stood in front of the mirror looking very formal. He combed his beard and strung the new gold watch through the waistcoat. The transformation was complete; he looked every inch the Victorian gentleman in the photograph.

Phil trotted down the stairs and into the living room. The sight was breath-taking. Everything was authentic and perfect in its tribute to Victoriana and in its replication of the Christmas card; the tree decorated accurately, the ornaments on the mantlepiece, perfect in every detail, and the fire burning in the grate beneath glowing red and inviting.

And Jo stood there, in a wide-skirted dress, hair back in a bun, hands held demurely together, eyes sparkling with excitement. She bobbed a curtsy.

"Well?" she asked in anxious expectation.

"You've worked wonders," he replied, looking around the room. It was then he saw the woman on the sofa. He gasped. "Samantha."

"Hello, Philip," she replied, her long bright-red hair swaying gently as she spoke. "I'm so pleased you remember me."

"You know each other?" Jo asked.

"Yes, we did business together for a while," Phil said. "Samantha worked for a supplier. You remember, we talked about her?"

"Yes, I think so."

"Fancy you running an antique shop," Phil said to their visitor.

"I had to make a living somehow after you got me fired."

"That's not fair," Phil objected, "I merely said we wanted someone else on the account."

"After I declined dinner with you."

Phil sensed his wife's hurt gaze on him. "I asked for an evening meeting because we were so busy. I reject your insinuation utterly."

"You reject all you want," Samantha shrugged, "I hardly care. It was fifteen years ago, after all. And little Jo here isn't all purity, are you?"

"What do you mean?"

"Still don't recognise me? You knew my name before, when you stole my father."

"You're *that* Samantha? I babysat you and your sister Jessica."

"I was eleven, you were seventeen. Not such a big age-gap now."

"But I was a child myself. I didn't know what I was doing, what we were doing."

"Maybe." Samantha stood up and approached an old box camera that stood on a tripod close by. "What a lot of coincidences. Come along, let's get you posed. One each side of the fireplace, like in the picture on the card."

"The card you sent?" Phil asked, assuming his position, and hoping that the whole thing would be over once the photograph was taken.

"Very good. Go to the top of the class," Samantha sneered. "But you're not as clever as you think, my boy."

"Can we just get this picture over and done with?"

"You see, Philip, my dear," Samantha purred as she placed her head under the black cloth at the back of the camera, "you really aren't clever at all. Would a clever man get so drunk at a party that his wife has to drive home, even if she's had more than a few too many as well?"

"I don't understand."

"Well of course you don't. The last thing you remembered was the party, wasn't it?"

"Yes, until I woke up…"

"Behind the wheel of a crashed car with a dead girl on the road behind you. Oh, you were the perfect patsy, weren't you? You took your punishment, and you've never driven since. But it wasn't your punishment, it was hers." Samantha's finger pointed directly to Jo. "She just moved you across behind the wheel and walked to the bus stop."

Phil reeled as if physically struck. He had to grip the mantlepiece for support, and he found himself staring at the mysterious card. There was something wrong – what was it?

"All those years you played the devoted hard-done-by little wife," Samantha said to Jo. "And all these years you've played him for a sap."

Phil squinted harder at the photograph. He knew that he was hearing the truth, but he was seeing something too, but what was it?

"How could you know?" Jo asked.

"When someone hits you at fifty miles an hour and the last thing you see is their face through the windscreen as you go flying over the top of the car, well it's hard to forget who that person is. You don't remember what my sister looked like."

"Jessica?"

"Yes, my twin sister. We were very close. We shared one mind, really. And you didn't even have the courtesy to recognise us."

"I'm so sorry. It was ten years ago!"

"So, you don't remember what the woman you hit–you killed–with a car looked like?"

"No."

"Well, I expect the whole evening was a bit fuzzy after all you had to drink," Samantha's mock sympathy was humiliating.

Jo turned to her husband. "Did you see the girl?"

"Her face was… gone when I went to check her," Phil replied, still staring at the picture on the fireplace. "You let me believe all these years that I killed her… I lived through that hell in prison."

"I panicked, I'm sorry."

"Time to take your places," Samantha interrupted. "Time to smile and say cheese."

Phil took one last glance at the photo and gasped in realisation. "Look, Jo! Look at the man's wrist."

"What is it?" she asked, peering at the image.

"It's my smartwatch."

"Ready? Watch the birdy," Samantha growled.

"No!" Jo snatched up the card and ripped it in half.

"What are you doing?" Phil asked, trying to wrestle it from her grasp but only getting one part. "We don't know what it means."

"You'll just be apart now instead of together," Samantha explained with a half giggle.

"Then I'll just destroy it for you," Jo said, dangling her half of the photo over the open flames of the fire.

"I wouldn't do that," Samantha cautioned. "I'm just offering life imprisonment."

Jo smiled. "I don't think so." She let go of the photo and it fell into the burning coals. Within moments, her smile of triumph turned to a scream of terror when a jet of flame darted out and her clothes began to burn, together with half the furniture in the room.

Phil tried to reach her but was beaten back by the flames. Smoke filled the room and he coughed and retched as Jo's screams faded and Samantha's laughter replaced them. Eyes streaming, he made blindly for the door, but tripped over a table and fell to the floor. With a last desperate change of plan, he crawled to the window and forced it open. The inflow of air fanned the flames, but he managed to struggle through and collapse onto the front lawn.

The whole house was ablaze, and he watched his world destroyed while the night around him was filled with flashing blue lights and sirens screaming. Firefighters ran hither and thither, but there was nothing to be done, other than douse the inferno and leave a smoking shell.

Phil gradually became aware that Carol was with him.

"Come back with me," she said.

"Thank you," he nodded meekly and let her lead him to her home.

"You go on inside, I'll be right there." Carol was being beckoned to by a red headed woman standing in the shadows near her driveway. While Phil dumbly complied, she went to speak to the mystery woman.

"Take this," Samantha said, handing over a piece of card. "If he ever causes you trouble, threaten to destroy it." She walked away into the night and became another shapeless shadow.

Carol went inside and examined what she had been given under the hall light. It was half of a ripped photograph featuring a Victorian gentleman who bore a passing resemblance to Phil. She almost threw it in the bin, but something stopped her, and she laid it to rest in the drawer of her desk.

The clock chimed midnight.

"It's Christmas," she muttered.

Fire investigator Fiona Miller worked methodically through the remains of the house. There was little to survey; most things were destroyed, and the cause of the incident was clear – the fireplace had not been satisfactorily installed and flames had been allowed to reach soft furnishings nearby.

She completed her notes when something caught her eye amongst the ashes. She picked it up. It was a greeting card featuring a man and a woman in 60s garb standing in their living room, and it said, 'Happy Valentine's Day.'

Most remarkable, that could almost be the living room of her own house as it looked when it was built, years before she was born. But it was such a fascinating picture.

There and then, she made her mind up. She would do a themed Valentine's for her and her boyfriend, and this beautiful card would be the centrepiece. There was an amazing retro shop on the high street that had opened up where that old antiques shop used to be.

S.J. Lomas is a cheerful Michigan girl who writes strange, and somewhat dark, fiction. She loves books so much that she not only writes them, but she became a librarian and a book reviewer. Her to-be-read pile is large enough to last several lifetimes, but she wouldn't have it any other way.

You can keep up with S.J. on Twitter @SJLomasAuthor, Facebook, Goodreads, Instagram or her website: www.sjlomas.com

BOOKS BY S.J. Lomas

Dream Girl

Dream Frequency

The Blue Muse

SHORT STORIES BY S.J. Lomas

Kiss of Death

Sick Day

The Holiday Party

by: S.J. Lomas

Marcy sat in the passenger seat of Nick's Jeep, twisting her gloves into a tight coil. The snowstorm wasn't the only thing making her nervous. This holiday party was the first time Marcy would be meeting Nick's oldest friends. They lived all over the country now and the annual party was the one time per year that they made it a point to get together. "To combat the stress of family holiday shit," Nick had explained.

"Hey," Nick said, reaching over to give Marcy's busy hands a squeeze. "Don't worry. You guys are going to-"

"Both hands on the wheel!" Marcy snatched her hands away and pointed at the steering wheel.

Nick quickly returned his hands to the 9 and 3 position.

"Ahh. So, you're more stressed by my driving than meeting the gang." The tone of his voice was light, teasing. He grinned, although he kept his eyes on the swirling mass of white and glowing red brake lights ahead of him.

"Sorry. This storm is definitely freaking me out. The forecast said snow. Not a disaster like this! I'll feel a lot better when we get there," Marcy explained, a little embarrassed by her outburst.

Even though he'd risked his grip on the wheel to reassure Marcy, she could see he was holding on with white-knuckled intensity. It wasn't easy to drive in these conditions and they still had a long way to go. The blower was on full blast, to keep the windshield defrosted and the two occupants toasty. The wind outside drove dense sheets of white flakes across the road, creating white out conditions. Even creeping along at 15mph, it still felt too fast for the icy expressway.

"Me too, but I'm so excited for you to meet Evan. My two favorite people will finally get to hang out with me. It's going to be great."

Despite the anxiety of the dangerous drive, Marcy couldn't help but smile at that. She knew Nick and Evan had been best friends since middle school. That was an amazing feat in and of itself. But when Evan had moved to Colorado after college, leaving Nick behind in Michigan, they had still managed to keep in touch. Marcy knew they talked on the phone a lot and she really admired the bond between the two friends. Perhaps it was because Evan and Nick were both single and most of her friends were married now, but she didn't talk to her old friends nearly as much as she'd like to. Sometimes, it made her sad, but other times she just figured that's how life went. You grew up, moved further away, made your own family, and slowly drifted apart. Maybe she should have felt more nervous about spending the weekend with Nick's longtime friends, but really, her heart soared with excitement and hope that she'd integrate in with everyone the way Nick kept assuring her she would.

After crawling another mile down the road, Nick broke into Marcy's thoughts.

"Okay, maybe the storm is stressing me out too," Nick admitted. "Would you mind putting on the holiday station? That'll give us something else to focus on."

Marcy reached over to fiddle with the radio buttons. When she heard the age-old tones of Burl Ives, she knew she'd come to the right station. It did calm her. The song always reminded her of her childhood, sitting in the backseat of her parent's sedan with her grandma. Every year, they'd go to the drive-through holiday lights display that went on for five miles. They'd put on the classic Christmas songs in their car and ooh and ahh over the elaborate colored light displays twinkling against the shining white snow.

Marcy broke out into song, along with the voice on the radio, to help dispel the tension. Nick glanced over at her briefly before joining in. If they didn't happen to know all the words to a song, they made them up on the spot, often making the other laugh uproariously.

Two long hours later, Nick slid into the driveway of Lena and Brian's house. Marcy let out a sigh of relief as she opened the door to be greeted by a face full of cold, wet, wind that took her breath away. It wasn't the greatest welcome, but at least they were off the dangerous roads. She pulled her hood up, bowed her head, and made a run for the front door. Nick grabbed a bag of presents out of the backseat and hurried to join Marcy on the porch. They stood stomping the snow off their boots until Lena opened the door and welcomed them in.

"I'm so glad you guys made it okay!" Lena exclaimed. "We were worried you'd been caught in that pileup on I-75!"

Nick and Marcy exchanged glances.

"Really? We didn't see anything," Nick said.

"Maybe we were in front of it?" Marcy asked with a shrug.

"Well, thank God you weren't part of it and you're here safe now. You must be Marcella. I'm Lena. So good to meet you!"

Marcy hadn't even finished getting her coat off before Lena grabbed her into a warm embrace.

At least Nick had been right. Lena was definitely making Marcy feel right at home.

"I'm getting you all wet!" Marcy cried, quickly pulling free of the hug.

Lena brushed off the front of her sweater and chuckled.

"Doesn't matter," she said. "I'm just so glad you're here. Who knew we'd get a blizzard like this just in time for our reunion?"

"The weathermen certainly didn't. Two to three inches, my ass!" Nick piped up, setting the bag of gifts in a chair by the door and shedding his coat and wet boots. "Is everyone else here? It was so nasty out, I didn't even notice whose cars were in the driveway already."

Lena reached out to pull Nick into a tight hug and the sound of hearty laughter erupted from somewhere further within the house.

"Everyone but Evan," Lena replied. "He said he'd fly into Chicago last night and rent a car to drive here. I figured he would have been here by now, but Evan never is one to show up on time."

"That's for sure," Nick agreed. He tapped Marcy on the arm for emphasis. "Evan always knows how to make an entrance."

Marcy removed her fogged-up glasses and polished them on the hem of her blouse to warm them up. Feeling more relaxed, now that the difficult journey was over, she breathed deeply of the comforting scent of Lena and Brian's house. There was a strong scent of pine and the mouthwatering tones of cinnamon and cloves.

"Mmm. Your home smells delicious!"

"Thank you. Brian made his famous mulled cider. We also have eggnog, my cranberry punch, and nearly every kind of pop and beer you could want. The kitchen's over this way. Please come help yourselves."

Nick put his fingers lightly to the small of Marcy's back and planted a quick kiss on her ear for reassurance. Not that she needed any. She was already feeling at home.

She followed Lena into the kitchen where she opted for a nice warm mug of the mulled cider. It smelled so good; she couldn't resist.

"Who was at the door, babe?" boomed a voice from an unseen room.

Lena shook her head at Nick and Marcy before calling back. "You could come and see!"

Marcy peered at Nick over the top of her mug as she took a long sip of the hot cider. It made a delightfully toasty trail down her throat to her stomach and radiated warmth from within. Just what she'd needed.

Nick grabbed a glass of eggnog and led Marcy into the family room where four others were already gathered.

"It's Nick!" A balding man in a green sweater jumped out of his recliner and rushed Nick before crushing him in a bear hug. The others followed suit and piled on layer after layer of hugs and laughter. Marcy stood off to the side to avoid getting squashed in the joyful reunion.

Lena came to stand next to her.

"This is how we are," she explained. "My husband, Brian, is the loudmouth in the green sweater. Luke and Emma are the delightful little couple who are laughing their heads off while they're trying to squeeze your boyfriend to death, and Kristy is the one who's trying to jump on top of all of them."

Marcy appreciated the pre-introduction introduction. It was nice to see the friends in context, just happy to be together once again. It felt all the cozier thanks to the raging storm outside.

Marcy sipped her cider while she watched all the hair ruffling, hugging, and laughing going on in front of her. She also couldn't help but notice the assortment of framed photos on the mantle. A hearty little fire was blazing, making for the perfect holiday scene.

Lena noticed Marcy gazing at the mantle. "Come here," Lena said. "There's one up there you need to see."

Lena and Marcy crossed the room while the rest of the group continued to catch up with Nick. Lena pulled down one of the frames and held it out to Marcy. "This was taken when we were in college. We haven't aged a bit, right?"

Marcy scanned the smiling faces in the photo and then glanced at the group in the room. Nick had a spiky bleach-blond hairstyle in the picture, very different from his modest brown haircut now. Spiky Nick had his arm around the shoulders of a guy with shoulder length rock star hair and a leather jacket. Lena looked a few pounds too thin in the photo and wore a pair of shortalls with a tight-fitting tee shirt underneath. Emma had a veil of brown hair down to her elbows and Luke was hamming up kissing her cheek for the picture. Poor Brian looked like he'd started to bald early on, but he was much thinner than he was now. College Kristy had a pink pixie cut that was in stark contrast to the blonde highlighted bob she wore now. They may have aged, but Marcy thought everyone looked happy and healthy.

"Is this one Evan?" Marcy asked, pointing to Mr. Rock Hair.

"Yep. It's not fair how beautiful his hair was."

"I was just thinking the same thing."

"Hey, you guys," Nick said, reaching through the crowd and extending an arm toward Marcy. "I want you to meet Marcy. She had to sing Christmas songs with me for two hours to get through the crappy commute and she is worth every second of it."

Marcy locked eyes with Nick and smiled as his happy pals moved away and opened their arms, gesturing for her to get in on the hugging action.

"I'll hold your drink," Lena said, putting the picture back on the mantle and reaching for Marcy's mug.

Marcy laughed and entered the warm circle of hugs. What a remarkable group of people! She didn't know them yet, of course, but she didn't feel like a stranger either. She thought it was going to be a lovely beginning to a very special weekend. But as all the bodies closed in around her, wrapping her in a friendly embrace, she was struck with a sudden chill and an impulse to run outside. She shivered, which Nick noticed right away.

"You okay?" he whispered in her ear.

"Yeah," she said, the urge to escape still strong. "I just realized I left my phone in the car and I promised my parents I'd call when I got here." She didn't know where the words were coming from, only that she had to get out of there fast.

"You can use mine," he said, reaching for the phone in the pocket of his jeans.

"No," Marcy said, pulling free of the group. "I'm so sorry, I'm acting weird, but in this weather, I really don't want to panic my parents. I'll be right back."

She hurried out of the room and back toward the front door. She stepped into her wet boots, flung her coat around her, and pulled the front door open. She practically jumped out the door and into a handsome young man, with gorgeous hair, who was just coming to the top step.

"Oh!" she startled, pulling the door shut behind her in surprise.

"Sorry," he said, holding up his hands. "Didn't mean to scare you."

Marcy's bizarre sense of panic immediately dissipated into the frosty air.

"Leaving already?" he asked with a mischievous grin.

Marcy exhaled, creating a steamy cloud that floated up and away.

"No. I just needed to get some air."

"Yeah, we can be a bit overwhelming," he laughed.

Marcy laughed too. "You're Evan. It's great to finally meet you! You look just like that picture from your college days. Same great hair! Lucky!"

"Yeah?" Evan chuckled, putting a hand up to his hair and running his fingers through it. "And you're the stunning Marcy I've heard so much about. It's a pleasure to meet you too."

Marcy's curiosity was piqued. For a moment, she wished she knew what Nick had said to Evan about her. Not that she could ask, but it was nice to know that he'd heard "so much." They'd been dating since January, approaching their one-year anniversary. She couldn't think of anyone she'd rather be with.

"Nick didn't tell me you had hair like that," Marcy said. "Let me guess, it's just naturally like that. I won't even tell you how long it took just to get my hair looking presentable." She reached up to pat her own hair, which was rapidly becoming damp with snow. Great. She probably looked like a wet dog. Evan's hair was so shiny and full, it looked like the snow was sliding right off it. Lena was right. It just wasn't fair. She pulled up her hood to get her hair out of sight and keep it from getting any wetter.

"You make it look effortless." Evan winked. "Am I the only one missing?"

"Well, you're here now. I think we're all accounted for."

"Indeed, we are."

There was an amiable pause and Evan gazed wistfully at the front door.

"Let me get out of your way so you can get inside where it's warm. You must be freezing." Marcy noticed that Evan only had a thin, black, leather jacket on. Like in the picture, but not nearly warm enough for weather this bad.

Evan shrugged. "I hadn't noticed. Anyway, I'm enjoying talking with you. It's nice to have a moment with my best friend's girl away from that madding crowd. They didn't bear hug you yet, did they?"

Marcy took a deep breath of the crisp air and exhaled another cloud of steam. "They did, actually, but I got this powerful urge to come outside. I kind of panicked and came running out here. Probably blew that first impression."

"Impossible. Nick's been talking about you so much. You've already made a great first impression on all of us."

Marcy was so surprised by his words that her embarrassment over running out completely disappeared.

"He has?"

"Oh, yeah," Evan agreed. "While we have this moment alone, I'm going to be frank with you. I've known Nick since we were kids and I can tell you with absolute certainty that he's completely fallen for you. He really loves you, Marcy."

In spite of the temperature and the snowflakes gathering on her eyelashes, Marcy felt a great warmth spread through her at Evan's words.

"He told you that?"

"You have a good heart," Evan continued. "I can tell that already. You and Nick are a good match."

Marcy blushed, even though her cheeks were already rosy from the wind.

"What a sweet thing to say!" Normally, Marcy would be skeptical of anyone who talked like that, but this was Nick's very best friend. She genuinely felt that Evan was speaking from his heart. She couldn't guess what he'd say next, but it was a surprise she was looking forward to.

Evan shrugged. "Life's too short to keep all the nice things bottled up inside. It's important to let people know they're loved."

"You know," Marcy said, getting a sudden spark of inspiration. "Nick told me he thinks of all of you like brothers and sisters. He said you've always been able to rely on each other, no matter what.

Especially you. I don't know if he ever says it, but he definitely loves you too."

"Thank you. It's a special group. I'm glad Nick finally found the right girl to join us." Evan smiled and slipped his hands into his jacket pockets.

"Oh," he said. "I nearly forgot."

He pulled his right hand out of his pocket and Marcy could see that he was holding a small, flat, box wrapped in gold foil paper.

"This is for you. Don't get too excited. It's nothing fancy, but I think you'll appreciate it. Don't open it now. Just hang on to it. You'll know when it's time to open it."

Intrigued, Marcy reached out for the box. She was hit with the sensation from inside again, almost like she was trapped and had to get away. But that didn't make sense. She was having a nice conversation with Nick's best friend. Her fingers brushed against Evan's for the tiniest instant and she shivered. His fingers were like ice. Surely he needed to get inside where it was warm. He'd catch his death standing out here in that thin jacket.

Once she'd accepted the box, the feeling passed. The gift easily fit in the palm of her hand, larger than a ring box but it had a little weight to it that ruled out jewelry. She was very curious about what Evan could have possibly decided to give her, more so because she couldn't open it yet. She was touched by the thoughtful, if mysterious, gesture.

"Thank you," she started but he waved away her polite gratitude.

"Just pop that in your pocket and forget about it until later. Like I said, it's no big thing."

"Nick told me everyone would be nice, but I didn't expect a welcome like this. Thank you so much, Evan. This is so kind of you."

At that, Evan smiled with such warmth that it almost dispelled Marcy's worries about his frigid cold hands.

"You're welcome," he said. "I think you're going to fit in very well around here."

Marcy slipped the little present into the pocket of her jeans, to keep it close to her, and stamped her feet to get the circulation going. Despite the delightful conversation, it really was unbearably cold. Marcy had reached her limit.

"Well," she said, "It's really cold out here. Should we go in?"

Evan looked at the door and then back to Marcy. He smiled but shrugged. "You go ahead. I left something in my car."

"Need any help?" Marcy offered, suddenly feeling like she didn't want this interaction to be over so soon.

"Nah. I gotta get it myself. I'm glad I got this chance to meet you."

Before she could reply, the front door opened and Marcy whirled around to find herself face to face with Nick.

"Hey, are you okay? I was getting worried everyone scared you off."

"Not at all. I've just been talking—"

"Argh! I hope you didn't call your parents yet." Nick said quickly.

Marcy gave him a quizzical glance. "No, I haven't called them yet—"

"Good. You'll have more to tell them in a little bit." Nick leaned in and planted a hot kiss on her cold lips.

Marcy wrapped her arms around him, all too happy to get lost in one of Nick's amazing kisses.

When they pulled away, she smiled at him. "What was that for?"

"Well, this isn't how I'd planned it, but you look so cute out here with your rosy cheeks and your hair all full of snow, I just have to do it now."

Before Marcy even knew what was happening, Nick knelt down on one knee in front of her, in the snow and slush on the porch, and he didn't even notice a thing.

"Oh my God!" Marcy covered her mouth with her hands as she stared in wonder at the man she loved.

Her heart was racing and her mind was an explosion of abstract images and feelings. If asked what she was thinking at the moment, she wouldn't have been able to answer.

For his part, Nick was giving an approximation of the romantic speech he'd practiced in his head for weeks. He wasn't quite sure what he was saying either. All he knew was that he wanted Marcy to be by his side forever, just like his friends had always been beside him.

Nick pulled a ring from his pocket, which he slipped onto Marcy's finger. Somehow a question was asked and a joyful answer was given. Marcy pulled Nick back to his feet and kissed him, and kissed him, and kissed him again.

It wasn't until she snuggled into his embrace that she realized they'd just left Evan standing there to witness this whole intimate moment. She turned to look but the porch was empty.

Had he known what Nick was planning and gone back to his car to give them privacy? Maybe he'd actually gone into the house through a back door? Before Marcy could ask, Nick kissed her once more on the forehead and took her hand.

"Come on," he said. "It's freezing out here. Why don't we go back inside and tell everyone the good news?"

Marcy glanced behind her again, just in case she could catch sight of Evan somewhere but all she saw was the steady falling of the snow.

They burst back into the house, shaking, and stomping the snow from themselves and laughing. They went back through the kitchen, where Nick grabbed a bottle of champagne from the fridge and they went back into the noisy family room.

"Everyone!" Nick announced loudly. "We have very important news!"

Marcy beamed at Nick and then looked around the room at the people who would be the first to know of the happiest news of her life.

"Marcy has just agreed—"

Lena's phone started ringing. She quickly grabbed it from her pocket and silenced it. "Sorry," she mouthed, but Nick wasn't the slightest bit deterred.

"To become my wife!"

Marcy held up her left hand and a roar of cheers went up around the room. Now that she was looking, she noticed that Evan wasn't among the friendly faces. Where in the world had he gone?

Lena's phone rang again. As Nick popped the cork on the bottle, Brian went to the kitchen to get the champagne flutes.

The friends came up to congratulate the new couple, but Marcy kept an eye on Lena's face as she took the call in the back of the room. With the phone on one ear and her hand pressed over her other ear, Marcy watched as Lena's face drained of color. Despite the feeling of warmth and mirth in the room, Marcy could almost feel a draft pass through. She saw the next few moments as if in slow motion. Lena ended the phone call and grabbed the back of a chair. She couldn't bear to stand on her own. Her face contorted into a deep grimace. She looked like she was screaming, yet no sound came out.

Marcy broke away from the well-wishers and hurried to Lena's side.

"What happened?" she asked.

"That was Evan's sister," rasped Lena, turning vacant eyes to Marcy. "He's gone."

Marcy shuddered, as if a cold wind had just passed over her.

"What do you mean?" she asked slowly. Even though she instinctively knew what Lena meant, it wasn't possible. It couldn't be.

"An accident," Lena said as tears began to form in her eyes. "Early this morning. A semi couldn't stop on the ice—" She could say no more. She didn't need to.

Marcy sprang back from Lena as if she'd received an electric shock.

"No," said Marcy, quietly, in disbelief. "That can't be. He was just—"

Marcy jumped up and raced once again to the front door. Without even bothering with her boots or coat, she threw open the door and ran out into the snow in her stockinged feet.

"Evan!" she shrieked. "Evan, where did you go? There's been a terrible mistake!"

She looked for footsteps in the snow, any indication of where he'd disappeared to, but there were none. Not even so much as a partially filled indentation that even hinted at footprints.

Nick raced out of the house, shocked by the news Lena had delivered as well as the dramatic behavior of his new fiancé.

"Marcy, what are you doing?" He tried to hold her and guide her back to the house, but she shook him off and tripped, falling into the snow.

"He was right there!" she wailed, pointing to the porch. "We were just talking."

"Who?" Nick asked, crouching down next to her.

"Evan! I met him when I came outside. He was wearing a black leather jacket and we were just talking. He wasn't in the accident. He's here!"

"But honey," Nick said quietly. "No one was with you when I came out."

"He said he left something in his car. He went back to get it and then you came out."

Nick glanced around at the snow-covered front lawn and driveway.

"There aren't any other cars here. Ours is the last one."

Marcy looked around frantically, trying to make sense of what was going on. There were no fresh footprints from the driveway. Indeed, there was no car to account for Evan. Not even tire tracks to prove that he'd been and gone. Even though the snow was falling fast and heavy, it couldn't have obliterated every trace of him that fast. Could it?

Marcy stared into Nick's worried eyes, trying to make him see that she wasn't out of her mind. How could she make him believe she was telling the truth? Finally, an idea penetrated the confusion in her brain. Even though nothing was adding up, she could prove that it was all a mistake. She frantically reached into her pocket and pulled out the box. There it was, wrapped in gold foil paper.

"This!" she practically screamed. "He just gave me this! He said I'd know the right time to open it."

Nick didn't speak, just stared at the little box in her hand.

She tore open the paper, as the rest of the gang came out to see what was going on with Marcy and how she could possibly be so affected by the death of their lifelong friend, whom she hadn't met yet.

She opened the lid of the box and discovered a tiny slip of paper folded into a little gift tag. It read:
Congratulations Marcy & Nick
Wish I could be there for your big day. Maybe you can have this there instead?
All the best, Evan

Under the card lay an old fashioned, small, metal, stopwatch. Nick was so shocked to see it that he nearly toppled backwards into the snow.

Although her emotions were running high in all directions, Marcy had enough presence of mind, to realize that the stopwatch was familiar to Nick.

"Nick," she said. "What is this?"

His mouth opened and closed, but no words came out. He couldn't deny that he'd seen that stopwatch before. He knew it well, although it had been many years since he'd seen it.

"You have to tell me," Marcy said. Her own hysteria calming, now that she had the proof that she'd just been with Evan.

"We ran track together in high school," Nick said in a voice barely louder than the snow falling to the earth. He reached out, took the stopwatch from the box, and flipped it over to the back, unable to believe his eyes. Sure enough, he found what he was looking for. Nick and Evan had spent countless hours trying to improve their run times. Both of them had held tight to that stopwatch while timing the other, to see who would be the fastest. The stopwatch had belonged to Evan, a gift from his father, who was so pleased that Evan was taking an interest in some sort of sport. But Nick, as best friends do, enjoyed "borrowing" the stopwatch because he only had a plastic one, and he thought this metal one of Evan's was cooler, and more accurate. To make sure his friend never permanently made off with it, Evan had scratched his initials into the back: EGP, for Evan Garret Palmer. Nick had drawn his initials on it with a permanent marker. Although most of that had worn off, there was definitely the remnants of his NMR, for Nicholas Michael Rogers.

The others rushed closer to see how this bizarre drama would play out, and hoping that the phone call Lena had received, was just a terrible mistake.

"I can't believe it," Nick said. "There's no way anyone else could have had this. It's definitely the same stopwatch Evan and I used in high school. Our initials are still on it!"

"I talked to his sister, Chloe," Lena said, her voice thick with tears. "It's not like she's going to call up and say something like that to mess with us. She could barely get the words out to tell me."

"There must have been some awful mistake," Marcy said. "Evan was just coming up the steps when I came outside. We talked and he gave this gift to me. Said I'd know when to open the box. I'm telling you. He was here."

Everyone stared at each other in disbelief, trying to figure out what could possibly be happening.

"But where is he now?" Kristy finally chimed in, attempting to be a voice of reason.

All eyes turned to Marcy.

Marcy racked her brain, trying to remember every word he'd said. "He said he forgot something in his car. I turned to come back in the house and Nick was coming out to propose."

"He wouldn't come all this way to give you a stopwatch and leave without coming in. That doesn't make any sense." Kristy tried to talk through her confused thoughts.

"But he definitely gave her this," Nick piped up. "There's no way anyone else would have this. Plus, there's this little card, in his handwriting. But I didn't tell him I was going to propose on this trip. I don't know why he said anything about our 'big day.'"

"What did he look like?" Emma asked. She stood with her head up, facing the falling snow.

"He was wearing a black leather jacket and looked just like he did in that picture on the mantle. I even complimented him on his gorgeous hair. It was just as glamorous as in the picture. Maybe even better."

"That's very interesting," Emma said quietly, still looking up at the sky. "Time hasn't been kind to Evan's hairline."

Now everyone turned to look at her. Always the quietest of the group, Emma was also quite sensitive. It seemed like she knew something.

"What are you saying? I wouldn't say something like this if I didn't believe it was true. I'm not trying to hurt you." Marcy cried as tears began to sting her eyes. She remembered the incredible coldness of Evan's fingers. How he didn't even shiver in that thin jacket. How the snow didn't cover him like it did her. How her breath made all kinds of condensation clouds and his did not.

"I'm not accusing you of anything," Emma said. "I believe you. I think Evan was here, but not in the way we were expecting. He wanted to meet Marcy to say goodbye."

Emma's calm explanation hung in the air like the breath Evan would no longer breathe.

Nick looked down at the stopwatch in his hand and blinked back his tears.

"See?" he asked Marcy. "I told you Evan was always good at making an entrance." It was too much then. Nick broke down and Marcy pulled him into her arms. There were no words to smooth over a heartbreak of this magnitude, but she loved Nick and shared in his grief over the friend she'd met all too briefly.

As Emma's explanation began to sink in, the group closed in tight to share a very different kind of hug than when Nick and Marcy had arrived. No one bothered to say anything. Not aloud anyway. But in their hearts, none of them would forget that holiday party the year of the accident, and how they'd all managed to show up anyway. If only for one brief, unbelievable, final time.

The Carolers

by: S.J. Lomas

Kenneth sat alone on his worn plaid couch with the squeaky springs. A microwave dinner perched on his knees, he ate lukewarm salisbury steak while bathed in the glow of his favorite game show, *Lucky You!* The small house was definitely old and well worn, not unlike Kenneth himself, but it was tidy. He knew how to keep things clean and in their place. It was a throwback to his Air Force days. He was a minimalist by nature and didn't believe in wasting money on possessions. Kenneth had what he needed, and that made him happy, more or less. As happy as a seventy-nine-year-old perpetual bachelor gets.

The thermostat was set for a brisk 65 degrees, just as Kenneth preferred it. Heat was a necessity in the winter, not a luxury, and he treated it as such. He didn't notice the chill much these days anyway. It was cold outside. Warmer inside. What more could he ask for?

Kenneth was planning to watch his game show until he was ready for bed, or until he fell asleep on the couch. Whichever came first. To save energy, and money, the only light on in the house came from the flickering glow of the screen.

Murphy, his black cat and companion of twelve years, jumped up onto the back of the couch and nestled into a dent just above Kenneth's head. Thus settled in, Kenneth mindlessly spooned food into his mouth and tried to solve the puzzles before the contestants on the screen.

The host smiled his way through the question, "What famous English author has written over forty—." The television made an electrical sizzling sound and went black.

"What the hell?" Kenneth asked around a mouthful of meat. The only answer he received was Murphy sighing in his sleep.

Kenneth set his meal on the coffee table in front of him and got up to investigate. He looked behind the flat screen as if he'd see a switch that needed to be flipped to solve the problem. There was no telltale visual cue to indicate the cause of the trouble, but he did detect a faint smell of static electricity.

"You're not on fire, are ya?" he rhetorically asked the television.

"No," came the tinny answer, followed by a laugh track.

Kenneth staggered back a few steps, nearly toppling backwards over the coffee table.

The blank screen betrayed nothing. Neither did the resulting quiet in the room. Complete silence was broken only by the methodical ticking of the wall clock.

"Must be an odd coincidence," he said, rubbing the back of his calves where he'd bumped into the coffee table. Surely, that was going to bruise.

"Answer the door." The television blared the scratchy audio at full volume, followed by an ominous crescendo of music.

Kenneth clapped his hands over his ears, convinced that there was some sort of electrical damage that was causing the audio to short out before the whole device died completely. He reached over to yank the power cord from the wall and a knock sounded at the front door.

Kenneth froze in place, the cord dangling from his fingers. No one ever knocked on his door. Even on the rare occasions when he invited someone over, they rang the doorbell. And what were the staggering odds that a line of sitcom dialog would seem to prophetically tell him to answer his door? If he mentioned such a thing to his young, hotshot, doctor, he'd probably start earnestly looking for signs of dementia.

The knock came again. Three short raps.

Murphy, startled from sleep now, jumped from his perch and ran away to hide in a dark corner of the house.

The house was tidy and cozy enough, but not large. What would a single man need with a large house? The front door was set into the living room, where Kenneth stood frozen. The kitchen to one side, the bedroom and bathroom on the other. From where he stood, still facing the television, the door was behind him. He didn't particularly want to open the door, his mind running rampant with all sorts of bizarre possible visitors. But still, had he really become a foolish old man? Just because his television was on the fritz, he was now too rattled to answer the door? The weather was wintry and cold. Could be someone needing help. Would he leave them shivering on the porch just because things were out of sorts at the moment? That was no way to live.

He dropped the cord from his hand and turned toward the door. It was a solid wooden door except for two half circle windows set into the top of it. Higher than a normal person's height, to allow in light but maintain privacy. He kept the porch light on when it was dark out, so he noticed the movement of fat, large, snowflakes tumbling past the windows. He stared at the snowflakes, thinking that he should move to answer the door, but finding that he was rooted to the spot.

One more time, the knocking came. This time, more playful — *shave and a haircut, two bits*! That was the standard knock his family had always used when they'd come to visit. Not that most could anymore. All he had left was a couple of nieces and a nephew who lived out of state and were too caught up with their own lives and children to visit an eccentric old uncle. He didn't begrudge them their lives. He was proud of them. But the familiarity of the less formal knock snapped him into action. He went to the door, counted to three in his head, and flung it open. Of all the things he might have expected to find on the other side, the scene before him was not on the list.

A group of seven huddled on his porch, bundled in hats, earmuffs, winter jackets, boots, and gloves. Each had a white scarf wrapped around their nose and mouth. Together with the hoods, hats, and earmuffs, only a strip of their faces were visible, and their eyes fixed on him. The yellow glow of the porch light made it appear like they were shining.

"Can...can I help you?" Kenneth stammered.

"Happy holidays, Kenneth! May we come in and sing a song for you?" Although the scarf of one of the visitors moved as though the person was speaking, the sound of the voice came from behind him! From the television.

Horrified, Kenneth turned back to stare at it, which the group took as a cue to follow him in. The last one in, a very fair skinned woman with eyes as grey as a storm, closed the door behind her and locked it.

Before Kenneth could say a word, the television offered more conversation. "This snow is gonna be a howler. You're our last stop before we go home tonight. Lucky you!"

Kenneth's heart thudded in his chest in an alarming fashion. He took medication to keep it from behaving that way, but this seemed to be too much for even science to quell. His legs felt weak and his head started to spin. His vision began to blur. With his tiny room full of strange carolers, the scent of electrical fire burned in his nostrils.

"You should sit down. It's okay, Kenny," said the voice of a young man from the television as one of the visitors stepped forward and gestured to the couch.

Despite his internal alarm at what was happening to his body, Kenneth realized that it wasn't the porch light at all that had made the people shine in the light. It was they, themselves, emitting a comforting golden glow. His blurry eyes couldn't make out any specific features, but the light was fantastic. How had he failed to realize that they possessed no color of their own, other than the glow? There were five pairs of grey eyes in five very white faces. Their clothing was greyscale. These contrasts of light and dark, were all he could make out of them.

When Kenneth made no move, two of the visitors came to either side of him and placed their gloved hands on his arms. He couldn't feel the weight of their touch at all, but it tingled deep within him, like a surge of electricity. The next thing he knew, he was sitting down heavily on his couch, in his favorite spot. His heart still jerked and fluttered strangely in his chest, but it was becoming a retreating thought in his mind. He was more drawn to his visitors, than to what was happening bodily.

"We've prepared a very special song for you, Dear," said a female voice, from the television again, of course. It was a young voice, but it disturbed a cobweb in the back of Kenneth's mind. Something about it was very familiar. Beloved even. He trained his eyes on the figure he thought it had come from, but it was impossible to tell who anyone might be from that little strip of white flesh and grey eyes. "Just relax and everything will be wonderful in a moment."

The group looked around at each other. Then, they fixed their gazes back on Kenneth and a wonderful harmony rose, clear and strong, from the speakers on the television set. But it no longer sounded tinny, and crackly, as if playing from an old gramophone. It sounded like his home had been transformed into the greatest concert hall and the sound resonated not just in the air around him, but throughout his body as well. Indeed, it was so beautiful, Kenneth had never felt more alive.

It took a few notes, but Kenneth recognized the song. Tears formed in his eyes. It had been so long since he'd heard it. Could he believe his old ears now? The song flowed over, around, and through him. A song he'd first heard as a very young boy. Sitting in the kitchen with his grandmother, she'd sing that song as she baked cookies for their family Christmas dinner. Even from a young age, it had been his job to stir the batter in her big mixing bowl with her ancient wooden spoon.

"This is our song, Kenny," she would tell him every year. "This is the song of our family. Handed down from generation to generation. It keeps the love of family around us, even when we're parted. By distance. By heartbreak. Even by death."

He'd been around the sun on this earth for 79 years, but he'd never really understood what she'd meant by that until this moment.

As his heart began to stutter more violently, his vision cleared, and the singers began to unfasten their scarves, one by one.

The first was a woman. Although he'd never seen this young, beautiful, face before, there was no mistaking her identity. This was Grandma June. Of course. She'd taught him the song, why wouldn't she be the one to lead everyone in the singing now.

Next, came her husband, Grandpa Ulrich. He'd been a reserved man in life, but gentle in his own way. Young and handsome, he nodded a greeting to Kenneth as he continued singing.

Kenneth stared with increasing anticipation as each new face was revealed: Grandma Maggie and Grandpa Joe. His own mother and father. Finally, his beautiful sister, Annie. It had been a hard five years since she'd passed. No one had ever understood him like dear, Annie had. His big sister, she'd always been fiercely protective of baby Kenneth. A habit that had carried her through life. Even when they lived in different states, she with her husband and children, and him, alone, as always, in his house. He wasn't the same after he'd returned home from Vietnam, but Annie hadn't expected anything of him. Her love and patience had been as abundant as he needed and he'd always been grateful to her for that.

It was so good to see them again that he wept, openly. His body ached to be surrounded by these people, the ones he'd always loved most of all. Their smiles were radiant as they sang the familiar carol.

Finally, Annie smiled and raised her arms to her brother. He could no longer feel the movement of his heart. The spin of dizziness gone and forgotten. As his body fell back on the couch, Kenneth, filled with the warmest, overpowering, sense of joy, rose up to join her. His voice was strong and clear now, blending with the others in the final chorus. There was no cold, no pain, no longing, no discontent in him anymore.

After the final note was sung, he pulled Annie into a long wished-for hug. As they finally embraced, Kenneth noticed that everyone was awash in color. Colors so deep and vibrant he didn't have words or frame of reference for them all. Everyone was young and strong, and he was too. Everyone took their turn greeting Kenneth with a loving hug.

"Are you ready to come home now?" Annie asked.

"I've been ready since you left me," he said.

Annie took his hand and squeezed it. "Just wait until you see this, baby brother."

The room was bathed in a dazzling explosion of light. Murphy meowed from the corner he had hidden away in and the television popped back into life.

"What an incredible show we've had for you tonight. We hope you'll tune in again next time. You never know when it might be your turn to hear us say, Lucky you!"

The house was back in darkness, as Kenneth had left it. The television would continue to blare on and Kenneth's body would continue to sit in its glow from his favorite couch. But Kenneth would never give another thought to game shows, microwave dinners, or the traitorous heart in his body. Surrounded by the love of his family, they'd finally sung him home.

Derek R. King is a poet, musician, and published author. He lives in Scotland, enjoys the great outdoors, good malt whiskey, art in all its forms, (particularly the art nouveau, deco, impressionism, surrealist, and contemporary periods) and photography.

You might spot him on a hill somewhere with his camera fist pumping and quietly muttering "Yes!" to himself if he captures a great image.

His poetry, which covers diverse topics, has been variously described as "emotive," "raw," "powerful," and "fun."

Derek has written several short stories of which *Defying Convention* is one. A collected works of his poetry and short stories with accompanying visual images in the form of photographs and artwork (yes, he does that too, annoying isn't it) is an early stage work-in-progress.

His main work to date has been the award-winning and acclaimed nonfiction Civil Rights era book, *The Life And Times Of Clyde Kennard,* which tells the true story of one man's attempt to go to college in those challenging times.

You can find out more about Derek's nonfiction book at the website https://www.clydekennardlifeandtimesof.com.

You can follow Derek on Twitter at @DerekRKing2 where you can find the occasional poetry and photo post.

Derek is also a supporter of IndieCall.org and Twitter's #WritingCommunity.

BOOKS BY Derek R. King

The Life and Times of Clyde Kennard

Defying Convention

By: Derek R. King

It was a crisp December morning when I threw back the curtains. A big, beautiful, blue sky with low yellow sun belied the true temperature outside, as I discovered when I lowered my gaze to the frosted leaf tips of the last vestiges of autumn clinging manfully onto branch and twig.

Ahead of me that day lay a 170-ish mile journey to meet friends in their relatively new home up north. Being well settled in now they'd planned "a little celebration at this happy time of year" as they put it, "to bring some friends together." I hadn't been back to their place in ages. I'd helped them with their renovation works a while back, and now they'd invited me back, which was kinda nice.

Although the weather was, quite simply, picture postcard stuff here, the weather forecast for where I was headed could not have been more different. It was pretty grim to be honest, with heavy snow, strong winds and blizzard conditions forecast. Hopefully, I'd skirt round it. That said, the Ministry of Fear, as I sometimes refer to them, can have a tendency to talk up the doom and gloom about the weather. However, with a busy work schedule and not wanting to take a risk with my own car on a long journey in that kind of predicted weather, I had decided to hire a car for this trip. It sat in the drive alongside my usual chariot.

Having equipped the hire car with the winter essentials for such a journey: antifreeze screen wash, flask of hot stuff, some food, energy bars and a blanket, I was ready to roll after breakfast.

With breakfast served, scoffed and dishes washed, I grabbed my leather overnight bag, house keys and car keys, eventually remembering it was the hire car I was taking. Opening the car's rear door, I slid my bag along the back seat and strapped it in. Yes, I strap stuff in. I can't be doing with it sliding around the seat when I'm driving round corners or the dull thud in my back when it jams between the front and back seats, and there were plenty of corners on this journey.

My companions this trip were the car's radio and some wintry Christmas music I'd brought along: CD's by Nat King Cole, Phil Spector, Sting and some Mediaeval Baebes.

I fired up the car and waited those few minutes for the illuminations on the dashboard display to die away or stay on flagging up some crisis needing dealt with. Soon they were all off, thankfully.

The early part of the journey was wonderful, hardly a car on the road in either direction, beautiful scenery with copper and gold coloured leaves adorning the few shrubs and trees at the side of the road that had managed to hold onto a little part of autumn. It had been unseasonably mild of late, temperatures in double digits some days, this particular day was minus 2 but rising, just a blip.

As I neared my destination the horizon opened up. The trees had all but disappeared and I could see a huge expanse of heather moorland stretching out far and wide as the eye could see, with only the silhouette of the odd solitary tree breaking the near flat horizon line. I could also see what the tree canopy had been concealing. The weather was indeed closing in.

I seemed to be in the bright centre of an arc of menacing dark grey cloud closing in on me. Way off in the distance, I could see that the level of detail I had been able to pick out was now less defined, made softer by a veil of rain or perhaps snow. No sooner did

I see the wet stuff closing in than I was in it, and it was getting dark too. Those December days are short.

Initially, I was driving into large, wet, slushy snowflakes with the familiar sound from the wheels of squishy slush, but that soon changed when I drove a little further on. I guess it had been snowing here for some time before I arrived, proper snow, and it was still falling and falling hard. There was no skirting around it now. The squishy slushy noise had been replaced by the "dull fidget" wheel noise of driving on compacting snow. The car's headlights simply made things worse. This was the Ministry of Fear's blizzard and I inwardly apologised to them.

Whether it was a car fault or my lifting off the accelerator due to the conditions, is hard to say but in any event the car came to a halt. Thankfully, or perhaps not, no one else was mad enough to be out on the roads that night.

I had supplies. I could stay in the car, but looking about, I was in danger of being drift bound. So, I decided to leave the car but, before doing that, I moved it on a bit further and off the road. That decision was affirmed when I spotted a farmhouse not too far away. There were lights on and it was still quite early at 9pm. No doubt the local constabulary would not agree with my decision to leave the car. So, I called them and tried to explain.

"Is your vehicle a hazard to other road users," was the considered reply.

"No, I've moved it to a farm's field entrance so it's off the road."

"Good enough sir, we will let the Roads Department know in case the snow plough comes across your car."

That last statement made me wince a bit, I must confess.

The farmhouse in the distance seemed closer from the car than it did now as I trudged knee deep through the snow that had fallen, but it was still worth trying my luck. I struggled on, each step one energy sapping step after another. By now I was cold, I was wet, and I was tired, so I stopped for a breather.

The lights are still shining out from the windows when I arrive at the farmhouse door. I knock and wait. The porch light comes on and a lady answers. She's dressed in jeans, a fleecy heavy checked shirt and sheepskin boots and before I can utter anything remotely sensible, she greets me with a concerned smile and says, "Well met traveller, come away in." Her black and white border collie yelps at first, looks me over, then whimpers after a little finger wag from its master.

She leads me into the small hallway then disappears for a couple of moments, reappearing with an arm full of clothing.

"These were my fathers," she announces. "I keep them in case I haven't had time to do the laundry. They're clean and they'll probably fit you." She looks me up and down before adding, "But may be a bit big on you."

She points to a side room, "You can change in there, but be quick now, don't want the cold getting to you or I'll have to come in there and help you." I'm truly grateful to cast off the wet cold clothes I have on and I manage the fastest change of clothing ever. I thank her, kindly.

She leads me into the kitchen, where the Aga range is on, doing its thing, so it's wonderfully warm. She motions to me to sit at the large wooden kitchen table with its centrepiece, a large cornucopia of fresh fruit.

"I've got some soup on. I'll get you some. Warm you up," she says.

The soup arrives in a wooden bowl. "They're better than pots on a night like this, they keep the warmth," she explains. I'm too tired for the science, but my fingers and hands certainly agree with her as the heat flows from the wooden bowl into them. A thick cut, warm, crusty slice of bread soon arrives to accompany the soup.

As she glides around the farmhouse kitchen, I take a moment to look around this room with its stone walls, copper pots and pans hanging from a wooden ceiling rack. Various crops also hang from the rack and wall hooks too: cereals, onions, garlic, as well as lavender and various herbs. "I'll be safe from vampires then," I think to myself. And then there's the obligatory big white rectangular porcelain kitchen sink. It's a wonderfully homely place to be and I am very glad to be there. She tells me her name is Kate and that she farms the land, which she inherited from her father, as a shepherdess by herself, and has done so for many years.

Judging by the various rosettes on the end panels of kitchen wall units I noticed, and a collection of metal and perspex awards scattered about, some serving practical functions as bookends and door stops, Kate is also an award-winner and must be well respected in her community.

When Kate joins me at the kitchen table, the inevitable question follows after the soup and bread: "What am I doing out on a night like this?" So, I explain.

"Ah, that's why you're out, I knew you must have a good reason to be out in this filthy weather," comes the reply.

This is the first time I've noticed Kate's face. I'd guess she's in her late 20's maybe early 30's, quite slight with a happy cheery face. I guess I must have been staring or have a quizzical look on my face as before I get the chance to say another word, she jumps in.

"I know, I'm not what you thought a farmer would look like, right?" she asks.

"No, no," comes my reply. "Not that at all. I was thinking about the heavy lifting folks associated with farmers and wonder how you manage." I wish the ground had opened for me right there and then.

A broad smile breaks out across her face followed by a hearty earthy laugh. "At least you're honest," she chuckles. "Listen, I can wrestle a ram to the ground so don't mess with me." She continues laughing. "Anyway, anything heavy needs done I just give one of the other farmers a call and we help each other out."

Kate offers me tea or coffee. I accept tea. "I'll give you camomile with some honey, I think you need it, and I hope you don't mind." "No, no. That will be wonderful," I reply, adding, "Thank you so much."

I hear the sound of boiling water, then water being added to a cup, the sound of stirring and the slurp of a jar lid. "That'll be the honey," I think to myself. After a bit more stirring, the cup arrives, Kate passes the large pot cup to me, and as I lean forward to receive it gratefully, our hands touch. I try to retract a little, but she holds me to. There's an awkward fidget and exchange. "It'll be alright," she says smiling gently. My hands are now on the pot cup with her hands around mine, "It'll be alright," she repeats. There is something quite strange in this touch. It's not electric, but it is something. There's a warm soothingness to it. "Is that even a word," I think to myself. It's a very comforting, gentle, and peaceful touch. Fearing the worst, I look into her eyes and she into mine. There is only kindness there. She smiles a reassuring smile. "It'll be alright. You should try to rest now." As she finishes that sentence, the Border collie toddles over to look up at me, doffs its head to the right, paw scratches behind its ear and then settles at my feet. "She'll keep your feet warm," the shepherdess says.

When I wake in the morning, Kate and the collie are gone. There's a note on the kitchen table. "Had to go out and tend to flock. There's tea and I've cooked you some bacon. It's on the Aga. There's bread in the cupboard, please help yourself. I'll be gone for hours but please don't feel you have to wait for me to return. Your clothes are clean and dry and on the kitchen table." It's a nice note but strange at the same time. I'm desperate to say thanks and show appreciation for Kate's kindness and hospitality, but I do need to be somewhere else.

I determine to send flowers, er no, I can do better than that. A hamper. I'll send a food hamper and flowers, I tell myself. I see a pinboard on the far-off wall and thankfully there's an envelope with the address of the farm. I make a note.

I'm surprised by what I see when I open the front door. The snow must have stopped and been replaced by heavy rain overnight. The temperature has lifted significantly, so only a few pockets of snow are left in dips, hollows, and drifts. "That'll be where Kate's off to. Check if any of the sheep are stuck in drifts," I deduce.

I set off from the farm and look back, I'm amazed how Kate survives in this remote area. As I leave, I suddenly realise I'm not as far from my final destination as I'd thought, but I am much later than anyone was expecting, and I can see guests already arriving. Decision time. Should I breeze through and end up having to explain last night's experience? Nothing happened, but no doubt there would be insinuation, even though I know the hosts well. It'd be a tease more than anything. Or should I mingle with the throng entering the building to mask my late arrival? It was a rough day, so I choose the latter.

I make my way as covertly as I can manage towards the small stone-built country house. It's not rendered as is often the case up here. The masonry was left exposed to show off the exquisite detailing. None of that elaborate mock gothic gargoyle nonsense though. Just good old-fashioned quality stonework with some lovely detailing above the double entrance doors. "The country pile" the hosts called it back in the day. It was an apt description at that time, until they fell in love with the atmosphere of the place and decided to restore it. That's when I became involved. They'd known me for a while, Jules and Simon, and when they decided to restore, they thought I'd be their guy and so it proved to be. We worked tirelessly on the project, and when I say tirelessly, I mean just that. Hard graft, pouring over plans and options and budgets often with a glass of wine and a cheese board to hand. Great days.

I pass through the main entrance doors unnoticed, so far so good. I make my way upstairs, to the guest rooms. Thankfully, Jules and Simon have kept the old custom in these parts, a sprig of white heather and a lovely handwritten note of the guest's name on the guest's bedroom door. Thankfully, the door to my room is not locked and I quickly freshen up and head downstairs.

I smooth around the ground floor where guests are congregating. A thumbs up here, a nod there, a raise of the glass over there too. There's a string quartet playing Christmas songs in the large bay window area, which feels like a fish out of water, to be honest. More formal than homey but, hey that's just my taste.

I make my way over to my favourite part of the ground floor, the stone wall, and in particular the stone hearth. So much care was taken with the fireplace lintel, including the selection of the stone itself.

"I don't want a perfect stone," was Jules express instruction.

"What do you mean?" I asked.

"I want it to be good quality, but I want it to have some character. I like it when there are lines through it. You know, like sediment, is it?"

"Yip," I replied.

"My friend Suzie had one with ginger bits in it, like rusty. She hated it. Made them take it out and replace it with a characterless drab slab."

"OK," said I.

"I do not want that," she added emphatically.

"Jules, that works for me," I assured her.

And here it is, this buff sandstone fireplace lintel with a coppery or "ginger" come "rusty" band running through it and little narrow dark grey striations too. It is, frankly, a natural masterpiece.

As I move towards it, I see Jules, in her favourite cobalt blue sequined cocktail dress clutching a slender glass of Prosecco and deep in conversation. By the time I arrive to pat the stone, yes, sad I know, Jules is joined by another woman wearing a classically elegant black cocktail dress. I can't see the other woman's face, but I recognise her from the back. I can't recall her name. I recognise the hair style though, mousey brown hair in a very distinctive tight pleat.

I lean back on the wall and survey the crowd. This isn't my league; these are Jules and Simon's set.

Real nice people. Movers and shakers, as the saying goes.

I'm now quite close to Jules and this other woman. They've shuffled closer to me to avoid a garish conversation that has arrived on their other side. Some bloated loudmouthed buffoon is spouting off about stocks and shares. I see Jules shaking her head and rolling her eyes in an "there's always one" kind of gesture as they move away.

"How you holding up, pet?" Jules enquires of the other woman.

"I'm ok, Jules," she replies.

"Must be three years now, sweetie?" Jules continues.

"Yes, almost to the day. Jules, I miss him terribly. I miss him so, so much. It really hurts," she starts to sob, her shoulders and body begin to tremble gently. I hear sniffling and assume the tears I cannot see. I want to intervene and pass my handkerchief over, but I've left it in the bedroom and butting into the conversation doesn't seem right in any case.

It isn't long before the sobbing becomes almost uncontrollable. Jules moves in to embrace her friend, kissing her on the head as her friend lowers her head into Jules's chest. "It'll be alright, darling. It'll be alright."

Jules passes her drink onto an acquaintance, and with both hands takes hold of the other woman's upper arms and moves her away from her chest so she can look her friend in the face. "You know," Jules says. "We all miss him. Sometimes, and please don't tell Simon this, he's not into this kind of thing, sometimes if I'm up late and maybe a bit tiddly, I swear I can feel his presence here."

Keen to test her friend's theory the other woman now begins to turn around. It's the slowest of all possible slow-motion movements. Her head bows again. Her eyes seem to be tight shut, as if willing her friend's experience to be available to her also. Slowly her hand reaches out, moving towards me, heading straight for my chest. I try to move, but I'm transfixed, rooted to the spot. Her fingertips are within the breadth of a butterfly's wing of touching my shirt when Jules adds, "John put his heart and soul into this place, Jenny." Jenny's fingertips reach my shirt, her palm raises up against my chest. She startles, looks up quickly, eyes now fully wide open. Our eyes meet, she draws a deep sharp breath. Jenny, I know that name.

The string quartet is mid-glissando. Something's not right. Something is definitely not right. I'm panicking, a flood of emotions flow through me, but I'm rigid. Jenny's hand passes through me to the stonework behind me. She bursts into tears.

"Can you feel him," Jules asks softly.

"He's here! He's here!" is Jenny's intense excited reply. "Jules... he's here. I was touching him, but...but now ... "Gentle tears roll from her saddened eyes, drawing down her rosy cheek. "If I hadn't been away three years ago and agreed to meet John here, I would have been with him that night and he might still be alive, or we'd have been together. I miss him terribly Jules, so, so much." Jules moves quickly to embrace and comfort her inconsolable friend, my wife Jenny.

And in these few moments, my world stops..............., for I am John Doe and I realise that I am no longer of your world.

Natalie Reeves-Billing is a Liverpool lass with a dark sense of humour, which often spills onto the page. She loves to write spooky, fantastical stories for young audiences, and dabbles in poetry, satire, and cutting-edge contemporary fiction.

Natalie spent most of her early career in the music industry as a performer and professional songwriter. This lead, almost inevitably, to storytelling.

She is an Arvon Foundation friend and a student of the Golden Egg Academy. Natalie is mentored under the Lloyds Bank SSE program, with her Bubs Literacy project. She is published in several anthologies with her poetry and flash fiction, including *The Writing on the Wall*, *Read Now, Write Now*, and is involved in several collaborations with fellow writers across poetry, song, and scriptwriting.

Connect with Natalie on Twitter @BillingReeves #WriteChickens

Go With the Wind

by: Natalie Reeves-Billing

In the Harding residence, joy was prohibited. The ban had been in effect for almost three weeks. Unspoken, but deeply palpable. I can't say things had ever been particularly light-hearted there. Joie de vivre had been lacking for some time. Yet still, a small Christmas tree, stood defiantly in the window, clinging to better times. But if it were not for that token concession, you'd be forgiven for thinking somebody had died.

And died someone had. Nana Bess, God bless her soul. The glue that kept it all together. And though it would be two years ago this Christmas, still everyone felt death's bitter sting.

The arguments began right after. Born out of pain, grief, and regret. It wasn't the cheeriest of places, oh no. Not by a long stretch. But recently, Nathaniel had noticed every tick of the clock, every scrape of a plate and every chew of the dry, tasteless meat laid out before them.

Charles Harding, master of this establishment, ran a tight ship. He was tall and gaunt with a withered leg. Lately, he'd taken to popping pills at an ever-increasing rate. They rattled about his pockets in expensive silver dispensers. Now and then, he'd grab a handful, and crunch them confrontationally between his crooked teeth. Always the first to leave the table, without pardon or apology. He'd slink off in the direction of his office, in a haze of yellowing smoke.

Eleanor, his long-suffering wife, wore a smile as disingenuous as her Christmas centrepiece. But, she meant well and filled in the gaps on which their lives were built, with a patter of faux frivolity. Seamlessly dusting over the silences.

And then there was Nathaniel, an easy-going youth with a curious mind. Hair of jet, skinny and fawn-like. A true Harding…at least to look at. But his soul and his heart were much more than that. Nathaniel knew things about the world that most adults never would. He saw things as they really were. He had his grandmother's eyes.

Nathaniel was the only child of Charles and Eleanor. Too young yet to comprehend deep-seated repression, for that's what it was. To hold onto hurt like a thief to gold. And, God forbid a Harding talk of matters of the heart or show any outward sign of weakness.

But where did this leave Nathaniel? Sensitive as he was, in every sense of the word.

Well, on the 23rd of December 1944, Nathaniel's weary young mind did the unthinkable and thought for itself.

It was dinnertime. The grandfather clock made quite a fuss of it. The family, already seated and positioned, were about to take their evening meal. The wireless droned, leaking seasonal concertos, brass, and static in equal measure…hardly audible at all above the resonating weight of the atmosphere.

Five painful minutes passed in silence.

Chink. Tick. Chomp. Sniff.

'How was school?' his mother asked.

Nathaniel jumped. 'Fine, thanks,' he replied, glancing nervously at his father, who hadn't bothered to look up. 'Mr. Simons gave us gingerbread, and we sang carols under the tree.'

'Humph!' Charles snorted.

Eleanor offered water.

'I do *not* need a drink, thank you very much. I'm merely expressing my disapproval. Modern education is turning society into blithering idiots.'

Nathaniel's enthusiasm withered on the vine.

'It sounds like fun, dear!' Eleanor said, gazing wistfully at her husband. 'Lord knows, we all need a bit of *that* sometimes.'

Charles laid down his fork; he'd barely touched the glazed pork. He headed towards a crystal decanter and poured himself a brandy.

Nathaniel watched his father limp back to the table. How thin he looked! How old!
Frankly, he didn't know how to feel. It's hard to be sorry for someone so hateful.

'Nathaniel, you look tired,' his mother whispered. 'Your eyes are so dark. Are you OK?'

'Stop fussing him!' Charles snapped. 'He's probably up to no good most of the night. It's what they do.'

Nathaniel stared into his mother's eyes. She gave him the look. The one that was impossible to hide from.

'I saw Nana last night.'

Charles dropped his dispenser with a crash, sending tiny pink pills skittering across the table. Eleanor recoiled, her body stiffer than Staffordshire stone.

'She was calling me,' Nathaniel said.

Charles was in the grip of a coughing fit. Through bloodless lips, he managed, 'Dear God, not this again.' More coughing. 'Nothing good will come from believing in that stuff.'

'But, Father, she was saying, "Go with the wind" over and over. I saw Lakeview. I think she wants us to go there.'

Lakeview. Wow, Nathaniel couldn't remember the last time he'd said that. All those holidays there, together, as a family, seemed so long ago now.

'Have you been snooping, Nathaniel? Reading things you shouldn't?'

Eleanor tensed. 'For goodness sakes, Charles. It's a dream! He's not seen your blooming letter…'

What letter? Nathaniel thought. But his father was wound too tight for questions.

'He's been eavesdropping!' Charles snapped. 'Putting his nose where it's not wanted. No wonder he's tired.'

'Father, I haven't seen any letters.'

Charles shot up suddenly. 'See what I mean? He knows all about it.'

'Charles, dear. It's normal to think of those we've lost near the anniversary of their passing. Nathaniel's obviously missing his nana. We all feel it at Christmas. You know how much she loved this time of year.'

Nathaniel shook with frustration. 'But Mother, it's more than that.'

'Shhhh, my love,' Eleanor whispered. But Nathaniel was in a Devil may Care, 'two-up-to-the-wind' kind of mood.

'BUT SHE'S TRYING TO TELL ME SOMETHING!'

Charles slammed his glass down hard against the table. Dark, pungent liquid spilled over the brim. He began to pace. 'So, let me get this straight. A dead woman is communing with you?' Charles said, shaking his head. 'The money I spend on private schooling, and they turn you into a total utter...'

'Charles, maybe you should calm dow—'

'And maybe *you* should get a grip on him before he ends up at Briar Hurst, with the rest of the nut jobs. Maybe *you* shouldn't be encouraging all this psychic hoo-ha.'

Eleanor's face twitched like Old Sparky in its heyday. 'But it's just a dream, Charles. Nothing more. Every kid dreams.'

'That may be the case, but not everyone feels the need to analyse them. Pulling them apart, then jumping to ludicrous conclusions.'

Charles headed for the door, confident he'd had the last word.

But Nathaniel wasn't letting him off that easily. Not again. Not today! It was Nathaniel's turn to be angry. Angrier, in fact, than he'd ever been before.

'WHAT'S HAPPENED TO YOU?' he bellowed.

Charles stopped dead. The tips of his ears glowed red.

Nathaniel regretted it immediately and changed tack. 'I mean… are you OK? Is it Uncle William? Have you had word from the front? Or is it Grandpa? I know you miss him.'

Charles spun like a man possessed, his dark hair sticking awkwardly to his sweaty forehead.

'And what business is it of yours?' he spat. 'If I needed counsel from a fourteen-year-old child, I'd ask for it!'

Nathaniel's neck twitched as he fought back tears. Who was this man? Was his father still in there?

He shot out the room before Charles could get the satisfaction of seeing him cry. He slammed the door, sending a tremor through the whole house.

'Wait, Nathaniel. Wait!' Eleanor pleaded. Her voice, small and muffled through the thick walls. When wedged between rock and hard place, trying to please everyone, failure was the only possible outcome.

Nathaniel faltered. He hated seeing his mother like this.

'Don't you follow him, Eleanor!' Charles said, extra loud for Nathaniel's benefit. 'That's exactly what he wants. Ignore undesirable behaviour. That's what we agreed. Remember?'

How could he speak to us like this? Nathaniel thought. What, because he's some big shot at the War Office, he thinks he can treat us like yesterday's leftovers?

Nathaniel pumped his fists, his mood black. He reached for the door handle, seconds away from confrontation.

'He gets it from my mother,' Charles said.

Nathaniel stopped, ears pricked.

'But she was a woman, given to flights of fancy. But Nathaniel?'

Silence.

Gentle rustling. 'No. There's no place in society for weak men.'

Nathaniel moved closer to the door, horrified to find it open a bit. Thankfully, no one noticed. Nathaniel pressed his eye to the gap.

'No matter how much you read that blasted letter, it's not going to make your mind up for you!' Eleanor said. 'I knew it was trouble the moment I saw the postmark. I should've put it straight in the fire.'

The pop of the decanter.

'I only wish you had.'

'Charles. Your drinking. Your moods. They're destroying us. It's not fair on Nathaniel. He's just a boy.'

'Fair? Phhh, he should've grown up under *my* father's regime. Listen, I'm not going to Lakeview, and that's that. Father and me...well, that ship has sailed.'

'Your father's not getting any younger, darling. None of us are. It'd be better for everyone if you'd bury the hatchet.'

'After what he said? *I'm* selfish. *I* wasn't there for Mother. He's the reason I got this bloody job. To watch over the apple of his eye. It's *him* Father really wants!' Charles spat. 'Brave, William. Fighting for his country, yet still found the time to write home. And now he's missing.'

His anger dropped so suddenly, you could almost hear the suck of escaping air. 'And even with me pulling every string in the book, I still can't find him. I'm the weak one, Eleanor. In his eyes, I'll always be. Poor Charlie and his dodgy leg.' He punched his thigh in despair.

'Oh, Charles. Do let me in,' Eleanor pleaded.

'Leave me be!' he shrieked. 'William is dead. We all know that.'

Charles lifted the letter and ripped it to pieces.

'And Father's dead to me too.'

The pieces fell like confetti, and Charles disappeared into his office.

Nathaniel was gobsmacked. How final adult arguments were! He and his friends fell out more than in, yet a simple football game could change everything. But, what he needed right now was that letter.

Mrs. Brown, the ancient housekeeper, was gathering up the dirty plates, sniffing and wheezing as she worked. She loaded them into a rickety old tea caddy and disappeared into the kitchen. His mother soon followed, heading straight for the pantry, safe amongst the pots, pans, and the cooking sherry.

His stockinged feet slipped across the wooden floor with the grace of an ice skater. He quickly gathered together all the pieces, and with fists full of balled up paper, he scurried off to his bedroom.

Nathaniel was desperate to reconstruct the mysterious letter. He laid the pieces out flat on his desk, a complex mosaic of swirls and loops. The letter was dated three weeks ago. His father hadn't thought to share that news.

Lakeview Manor
Addington
Cheshire, SK9 5RZ

1st of December 1944

Dear Charles,

I hardly know where to begin. I've written this letter a thousand times, and none are even close to capturing the gravity of my feelings. I miss you, son. I miss you all. Terribly.
Our time is marching on, and we're powerless to stem its flow.

Please, come to Lakeview this Christmas. I know we can fix this.

I will be at Addington Station at 10am on the 24th of December. Good old Ray has agreed to drive. Alas, my eyes aren't up to it any more.
I beg of you, Charles, don't dismiss it out of hand. Life is fleeting.

Yours in hope,
Your loving father,

Thomas

The 24th? But that was tomorrow!

Nathaniel didn't have much time. He spent the evening sneaking about, gathering apples, cheese, a flask of milk, anything that could keep him alive on the long, cold journey ahead.

He raided his savings, putting the notes carefully in his trousers. Jumpers, underwear, pyjamas, soap. The trunk groaned under the strain. It took a lot of squashing and bouncing to close it.

And as dog tired as he was, he hardly slept a wink. He'd never attempted anything like this before. But there's always a first time. And at five forty-five, right before the housekeeper arrived, Nathaniel slunk out of the front door and into the dark morning. Streetlamps glimmered, and festive trees twinkled in neighbouring bays. Happy families tucked in tight in anticipation of the holy day.

Nathaniel took one look back at number ten, basking in the shadows of the overgrown hedges. 'Merry Christmas, Mother,' he whispered. 'And Merry Christmas, Nana,' he added, for there she was, standing by the gate, smiling from ear to ear.

Despite the trouble he would be in, Nathaniel enjoyed the changing view through the steamy carriage windows. Brick and slate gave way to grass and stone, as they ventured into a grand expanse of unspoiled wilderness. High above him, the sky was plotting. Mischievous and brooding.

Hours flew by in a haze, and by the time he reached Addington, the fecund clouds unveiled a whitewashed new world.

Nathaniel had barely stepped on the platform before a ruddy-faced man in a flat cap relieved him of his luggage.

'God strewth, Nathaniel. You've grown.'

Ray Cartwright. Gardener and widower. A permanent fixture at Lakeview. He lived alone in an old lodge house at the edge of the estate. A solitary man by nature. Mostly kept to himself.
'Ray!' Nathaniel flew at him, burying tears of relief in the sleeves of his tweed jacket.
'Come on. We're gonna catch our death 'ere.' Ray said, ruffling his hair. 'Yer father still in the carriage?'

Nathaniel froze. He didn't like lying, but the truth would have him back home faster than he could say collywaddle.

'He didn't come,' Nathaniel muttered.

Ray understood the complexity of the situation and didn't press further.

'Well, I'm sure yer grandpa will be just as glad to see *you*.'

Ray opened the gate with his boot and retraced his footprints towards a clapped-out Austin with the thinnest wheels he'd ever seen. Nathaniel was surprised to find it empty.

'Where's Grandpa?'

'Oh, he's bin burning the midnight oil. I knocked past earlier, but no answer. Yer know wot he's like. He's probably bin overdoing it in the garden. He'll have the kettle going by the time we get back.'

'You don't think he'll be too disappointed Father's not here?'

'Wot? Balderdash. He wuz more worried of no one showing up at all. He's had this arranged for over a month now. Got me to write it down and everythink. This is important to 'im.'

After much clunking and lever pulling, the ancient chariot spluttered into life. 'Ethel wuz always on at me to get rid of this old thing,' Ray said, patting the steering wheel, 'but thee don't make 'em like this no more.'

And probably for good reason, Nathaniel thought. The cabin was colder than the air outside.

'She'll warm up in a jiffy.' Ray said. Unfortunately, she never did.

The short journey to Lakeview wasn't a comfortable one and didn't feel all that short either. The seats were little more than benches, and the road, now covered in snowfall, hid a multitude of angry and rather deep potholes. The world outside was a giant snow globe, grainy and pixelated.

Soon the gates of Lakeview loomed, and the frozen lake brought visions of happier times. Picnics. Punting. Stickleback fishing.

The formal gardens. The covered pass. The army of limbless statues from the pages of Greek myth. Then, there she was. Lakeview. In all her beauty. A grand construction, full of detail and drama. You could gaze at her for hours and still discover something new.

'Ah! See! He's got a fire going,' Ray said.

Thick, healthy smoke belched from the tallest stack. 'The door's ajar. Get yerself in, and I'll leave yer things in the porch.'

'Aren't you coming in?'

'No. No. You guys 'ave got some catching up to do. But I'll expect a place for me Christmas dinner, mind.' Nathaniel's heart pinched. A Christmas without his mother.

'See you tomorrow, Ray. Thank you.'

Ray doffed his cap, jumped in the car, and trundled off in the direction of the greenhouses. Now, utterly alone, Nathaniel didn't feel quite so confident. His grandpa wasn't going to be pleased to hear he was harbouring a runaway, especially with things the way they were.

'Grandpa?' Nathaniel said, his voice so pathetic in the cavernous space. Snowflakes whipped at his legs, and he slammed the door quickly.

'Go with the wind,' a gentle voice whispered in his ear. But Nana was nowhere to be seen.

The scent of lily and lavender filled his nose. So familiar. Calming, somehow.

'Grandpa, it's me. Nathaniel.'

A stack of beaten up travel cases stood at the end of the corridor, a rifle propped up behind them. A smart green cap, with a bright red stripe, sat proudly on top.

Deep inside the house, angel voices spilled out of the old gramophone, accompanied by harp and clarinet.

'Nathaniel?'

Nathaniel's breath caught in his chest.

'Father?' But as the form came slowly into view—the pins, the badges—he realised the truth.

'Uncle William!!' he shouted.

'Little Nathaniel! Get yourself over here…'

Nathaniel fell into him, pressing his face tight against his uncle's chest, the material rough beneath his cheeks. A blend of sulphur, cigars, and polish. 'But, we thought you were…'

'It seems God has other plans for me.'

'Where have you been? Why…when…,' Nathaniel couldn't get his words out fast enough.

A cloud passed over Uncle William's face. 'I…I…'

'Woah, slow down, Nathaniel!' someone said, from behind him. 'And come here and give your old grandpa a hug.'

Nathaniel turned. Grandpa. Two long years hadn't changed him one single bit! In fact, he seemed healthier than ever.

The wire-rimmed glasses. His whitey-grey hair with a perfect wave. The woollen jumpers that made Nathaniel's eyes go funny. And the ivory cane with the eagle's head. Every concern he carried dissipated into the ether.

And in the doorway, Nana smiled.

In the warmth of the drawing room, all worries fell away. The hours flowed like a bubbling creek, moving happily from one topic to the next. The scent of fresh flowers hung in the air. The magnificent stone fireplace, its flames nipping at dry wood, festooned on both sides with garlands of evergreen and rich winter berries. A tall fir tree twinkled in the bay window, decorated with memories of Christmas past. The crude wooden angel Uncle William made as a boy, and the glass bauble Nana picked up at the Christmas markets. Symbols of love and remembrance.

In the warm glow of that place, it was hard to have a care, surreal, and dreamlike, as it was. The niggles inside blunted like a dull blade. Together, they sat in sumptuous armchairs, surrounded by photographs of loved ones past and present.

'Oh, Nathaniel. It's a tricky thing, time,' said Grandpa. 'You get so much of it at first. Days are years. Hours are days. And when you get older, and finally get around to understanding it all, there's so little of it left to do anything with.'

'Well, that's cheery,' laughed William.

Nathaniel saw an opening. 'What did happen between you and Father?'

Grandpa removed his glasses.

'It's my fault. Don't blame your father. My eyes were open, but I saw nothing. I ignored the man he was. Tried to turn him into me. Into something I understood. Into *my* father, and his before that.'

Grandpa picked up a photo of Nana.

'I did the same to her, too. My Bess. And still, her love for me never faltered. I loved her the best I could.'

'It's natural to miss those we love,' William said softly.

'That's what she used to say. "When your heart is heavy, that's the weight of their love living inside you."' Grandpa's lip quivered, and Nathaniel looked away. 'Your nana saw the world differently,' Grandpa said. 'She saw true meaning in everything. I wasn't willing to listen then. And now she's gone.'

'I don't think anyone truly goes, Grandpa. Not really,' said Nathaniel. 'I know Nana's here with us.'

Grandpa smiled. 'You've seen her, haven't you? You've got the eyes.'

Nathaniel nodded. 'I think she brought me here. Do you see her, too?'

Grandpa, eyes filled with liquid crystal, said, 'I don't see her, per se, but I feel her.' He stroked Nana's face and put the frame on the side table.

'I feel it too,' William said. 'I don't know how. Lord knows I've been so confused lately.'

Nathaniel wanted to ask so many things, but his Grandpa interjected.

'He's had a rough time over there, Nathaniel. He needs time to adjust.'

'Yes, it's all a blur,' William said. 'Rotten luck, hey? Sent home just as the tide begins to turn in our favour.'

Nathaniel nodded. 'Uncle William, has anyone sent word to Father? About your return, I mean. Father's been beside himself for months. We all have.'

'Don't worry. I'm sure they've sent word by now. If I know my brother, he'll already be on his way.'

Nathaniel's stomach twisted.

'Everything OK?' Grandpa said. 'You look like you've seen a ghost.'

'Yep,' Nathaniel lied, guilt burning in his chest. His father was going to be furious. But, perhaps seeing William, alive and well, would absorb the lion's share of it.

'Who knows, we might be together for Christmas, after all,' said Grandpa. 'And what a blessing that would be! Bess wanted that more than anything.'

'Mother loved Christmas,' William said. 'On Christmas Eve, she'd vanish into the kitchen. Wouldn't let a soul inside. We needed a crane to carry out all the food on Christmas day.'

Grandpa laughed. 'And those blasted movies she loved so much.' He stared fondly at the projector on the other side of the room. 'Some of them were over four hours long.'

'Not that you'd know,' William sniggered. 'You were asleep before the end of the opening credits. We had to watch in half-hour segments. A movie was a weeklong affair.'

Nathaniel giggled. 'The last time we were together, the last time I saw her, she made us watch that dreadful romance. Oh, what was it about again…?'

'The US civil war? Mother's favourite, that one. I sat on one side, feeding her handkerchiefs, and Charles on the other, throwing them in the bin.'

'Gone with the Wind,' Grandpa said, snapping his fingers. 'A truly depressing watch.'

Go with the wind…. Gone with the wind? Is that what she was trying to say? thought Nathaniel.

'Do you still have it, Grandpa? Could we watch it tonight for old time's sake?'

'I don't see why not. You'll have to get it all working, though. It's a tiresome fiddly thing. My eyes aren't what they used to be, and my arthritics are up to no good.'

'I'll get started.'

'The reels are in the cabinet.'

'On that note, I'm going to change into something more comfortable,' William said.

'And I'll get the kettle on,' said his grandpa. 'Reconvene at seven thirty?'

'Perfect,' said Nathaniel.

With William and Grandpa gone, Nathaniel glanced around. 'Hear that, Nana? Seven-thirty, it is.'

He settled down beside the large, cumbersome monstrosity. A steam-powered bicycle turned on its side.

'That is, if I ever figure this out!'

It was eight o'clock when Nathaniel finally beat the machine into submission. By the eerie light of a projection beam and the combined glow of fire and fir tree, they settled down to watch.

Nathaniel and his grandpa sat together, snuggled under one of Nana's patchwork quilts. Uncle William, in slippers and a dressing gown, sat in an armchair, nursing a glass of whiskey.
The air smelled strongly of spiced berries, a scent Nathaniel's mother loved so much. And as the credits began to play, a seed of doubt grew within him.

'I have a confession to make!' Nathaniel announced.

'Ooh, I love a good confession,' his uncle said, playfully.

'This wouldn't be something to do with your being here, would it, Nathaniel?'

'Well, actually…'

'It's quite alright,' his grandpa said. 'I knew Charles wouldn't come. He's stubborn like his old man. But you are Nana through and through.'

Nathaniel gasped. 'So, you knew all along? About my running away? Oh, I've made everything worse, haven't I?'

Uncle William laughed. 'Charles is a buffoon sometimes, but I can handle him. Relax. We'll be together for Christmas, and all this bad stuff will be behind us.'

'Hear, hear!' laughed Grandpa. 'Now, drink your chocolate and shut up, will you? We're missing the movie.'

Everyone laughed, and Nathaniel felt a wave of joyous relief. He drained the chocolate dregs and sunk into the cushions.

Scarlett O'Hara was on her second child and the proud owner of a sawmill when Nathaniel's eyes began to droop. He'd never quite understood what the film had to do with wind. Or what in particular was gone, but as he deliberated, he started to feel sleepy. He shook his head and tried to focus, but his tiredness was unrelenting, wrapping him tight in its fuzzy, warm folds.

As the colours began to blur, Nathaniel saw Nana on screen. Love and war played out behind her. Such depth and vibrancy. So real. So live. Like a mirror to another world. A room behind the stone wall. He wanted so much to go there. He lifted his heavy head.

A cooling hand, cold as ice, brushed lovingly across his cheek, and soft covers swaddled him. 'Not yet, Nathaniel,' it said.

Nana was aglow. A brilliant ball of energy. Raw and endless. Shadows stood before her, thin and long. Moving into her luminescence, further and further, until it consumed them. And by the light of dying embers, Nathaniel fell fast asleep.

Brack! Brack! Brack! Brack! Brack!

Nathaniel leapt off the sofa, heart pounding. The cold hit him like a brick wall.

'Grandpa! Uncle William!' he shouted, struggling to pull together the threads of reality.

The projector stood lifeless in the centre of the room. Tracks and fingerprints ran through the thin layer of dust that coated it. The fir tree had shed its pines overnight. They lay, brown and brittle, at its feet.

Brack! Brack! Brack! Brack!

'Grandpa! Someone's at the door.' Nathaniel was shivering as he ventured out into the corridor.

In the new light of day, Nathaniel could see how neglected the place really was. Obviously, Grandpa couldn't keep up any more. Bouquets of dead flowers hung limply over mounds of withered petals. Letters and packages were scattered on the doormat, and shadows moved through the frosted glass of the porch windows.

Nathaniel's heart plummeted deep into his bowel. This was it! He took a deep breath, closed his eyes, and opened the door.

He hadn't a chance to get a word out before arms were flung about his neck. Lips kissed desperately at his hair, his eyes, his forehead.

'Nathaniel, dear God, Nathaniel. There you are.'

Nathaniel opened his eyes. His mother and father knelt before him, and Ray stood anxiously in the wings. Their eyes were fixed on him. Full of worry and care. Was it really them?

Through undisguised tears, Charles said, 'Merry Christmas, son. I've been such a fool, and I'm going to spend every minute making it up to you. I promise you that.' Love welled in Nathaniel. 'But right now, I need to speak to your Grandpa.'

Nathaniel's brain struggled to compute. This was everything he'd ever wanted. The best present ever. Yet, the room was full of dense clouds. Expectant and prickly. Why?

'He's not up yet.'

'Nonsense. He's probably in the garden already. I must speak to him. Urgently.'

'They were up till late,' Nathaniel replied. 'Had a few night caps before bed.'

'They?' Eleanor asked.

'Grandpa and Uncle William, of course. Haven't they told you?'

Charles gasped. 'Who? Told us what?'

'The War Office. Uncle William's alive!'

Eleanor sagged, and Charles caught her quickly.

'What are you at, Nathaniel?' he said. 'Stop this at once. I got the letter last night.'

'What letter?'

'It's your Uncle William.'

Charles swallowed hard. 'He's dead.'

I've woken up in a parallel universe, Nathaniel thought. Where nothing makes sense.
He remembered his dream. Nana. The lights. But it wasn't clear enough to hold onto and faded the more he tried.

'Well, there's been a mistake,' Nathaniel said. 'We watched *Gone with the Wind*. Drank, ate, talked. He's alive.'

Eleanor broke into tears. 'What's going on, Charles? Can any of this be true?'

Charles shook his head in mystification and stormed up the stairs. Ray ran deeper into the house. 'Thomas!' he bellowed, opening the back door.

'Father!' Charles shouted from somewhere above. He moved from room to room, slamming doors with increasing agitation.

Nathaniel slumped in a chair. He couldn't think. Couldn't make anything connect. His mother knelt beside him, her face pressed close to his, breathing him in.

'It's awfully cold here,' she said. 'Doesn't grandpa heat the place any more?' Nathaniel couldn't answer.

He didn't know how long they sat there like that, waiting, drifting, holding on, before Ray's voice sounded. 'Charles. You'd better come.'

Above them, Charles's boots hammered, as he headed towards the stairs. And something snapped inside Nathaniel. He sprang out the chair and out the back door. Towards Ray's voice. Followed the footsteps through the snow, around the frozen greenhouse, and through the gate. Father was on his tail, shouting, begging. But it was white noise.

Ray knelt at the edge of the allotment, his back covered in snowflakes.

Nathaniel threw himself to the ground, crawling on all fours, trying to get a better look.

'Grandpa!' he screamed, his hands clawing at freezing snow, crushing it between his helpless fists.

'Nathaniel, this isn't for you!' Charles roared, pulling him up hard, and pushing him towards his mother. 'It's not for your eyes. Go! Now!'

'Grandpa!'

Eleanor caught hold of his arm and dragged him away, both of them howling. Both of them broken. Nathaniel pulled, but his mother was so strong.

Nathaniel's eyes pulled in everything they saw. Etched it into his heart. Father. His face wet with tears. Ray, hat-less, his shoulders shaking. And his grandpa, skin blue against the snow, laying awkwardly across the frozen earth.

The coroner's car pulled up an hour later. No one remembered much of the in-betweens. The death was recorded and noted down in triplicate on formal-looking paper. The 17th of December was his best guess, given the weather conditions. But that left some difficult questions.

Ray fussed about lighting fires and making tea. He hadn't seen any cars toing and froing, or anyone on the land who shouldn't be. And with no sign of Uncle William or his packing cases, Nathaniel had to accept he was probably insane.

The funeral directors collected Grandpa's body and left an emptiness behind them. Brandy bottles emptied, and lunch dishes were returned to the kitchen untouched. Nathaniel was fidgety.

He walked across the room, ran his hands over the walls, over the very place Nana had stood the night before. The surface was rough and cold beneath his fingertips. What should I do, Nana? he thought.

'Gone with the wind,' a voice said softly.

Lilies and lavender, as strong as a summer garden. The air was thick with it. And Nathaniel knew. He just knew what he had to do.

'Gone with the Wind,' said Charles, who hadn't said a word for hours.

Nathaniel spun around. 'Why did you say that?'

'Because I heard it,' he whispered, soft in his vulnerability. 'I know she's here. I can feel it.'

'Flowers,' Eleanor gasped, sniffing the air. Nana's presence was boundless. She was living in every atom of the house.

Ray crossed himself and muttered something under his breath.

'Nana brought me here for a reason,' Nathaniel said. 'And I think I know why. There's something I need to do. Christmas isn't over yet. So, Father, if you ever trusted me, trust me now.'

Charles nodded sadly. 'What do I do?'

It took only a few minutes to boot up the projector. Charles had a lot of practice. He worked fast, threading and winding, and Nathaniel turned on the power and lowered the screen. Eleanor and Ray closed every curtain and shutter they could find until the room was dark and shadowy. The family held their breath, as Nathaniel flipped the button, sending the ethereal beam onto the white screen ahead.

No one dared say a word, as the credits came and went. The familiar house, with its straight lines and symmetry, came into view and no sooner had Ms. O'Hara appeared, the picture began to change. Contorting and bending. Twisting and stretching. The image was transforming into something else entirely and expanding at a curious rate. As the colonial house faded, walls and chairs, tables and tapestries, quickly took its place. Impossible depth and resolution. A room opened up before them, a gateway to another world. A world, it seemed, not too dissimilar to this one.

Quite naturally, the family had drawn together, united in hope and amazement. They peered cautiously into the void, eager for a glimpse of this strange, new place. There was a burning fire, silver candelabras, and a huge tree glimmering in the centre of the room, littered with presents and trinkets.

Triumphant music spilled across the breech, and the scent of roasting meat and succulent gravies closely followed. Somewhere, just out of sight, happy voices rejoiced. Laughter and frivolity so pure and heartfelt, that Nathaniel was drawn like a moth to flame. Plates scratched, and glasses clinked.

And before they knew it, they had crossed the precipice.

Never had the air been so charged with love. In fact, never had there been a feast quite like it. The long table was lined with loving faces. Grandpa at the head in his paper crown. Nana and her knitwear. Her soft grey tresses tickling her shoulders. And Scotty. Their faithful terrier, sniffing for scraps as per usual. Uncle William still managed to look formal in a ridiculous Christmas jumper.

And, what a wondrous surprise for Ray, who sat next to his darling wife Ethel, blowing party horns in her ears. Charles and Eleanor looked at least ten years younger in the glow of family and friendship. Nathaniel absorbed it all. Quiet. Contented. A special place just for them. Made with love by those they loved. The strongest, most mysterious force in the universe.

Nana raised her glass.

'Thank you, Nathaniel. For helping them cross over.' She said lovingly, squeezing Grandpa's hand. 'And for bringing us together again. May everybody know the true meaning of Christmas.'

Nathaniel knew.

That's why his smile was so big. One of the most important lessons of all. Christmas isn't a time of year. It's a place in our hearts. And if we live in love, we will always be welcome there.

Printed by Amazon Italia Logistica S.r.l.
Torrazza Piemonte (TO), Italy